I don't really love sex . . .

I mean, I do. I love the thrusting, raw, power-ful energy that two people create when they're really losing themselves in a moment, driven toward one single purpose of pure visceral satisfaction. Even more than that, though, I love the electric, tangible, skin-tingling energy that two people create when they want it more than anything—but can't.

Seduce Me

By Dahlia Schweitzer

SEDUCE ME

DAHLIA SCHWEITZER

Seduce
Me

red

AVON

An Imprint of HarperCollinsPublishers

This book was originally published as *I Don't Really Love Sex (Sex mag ich eigentlich gar nicht)* in Germany by Maas Verlag in October 2005 and in trade paperback by Avon Red in December 2006.

AVON RED
An Imprint of HarperCollins*Publishers*
10 East 53rd Street
New York, New York 10022-5299

Copyright © 2005, 2006 by Dahlia Schweitzer
ISBN: 978-0-06-136348-1
ISBN-10: 0-06-136348-0
www.avonred.com

First Avon Red mass market printing: July 2007
First Avon Red trade paperback printing: December 2006

Avon Trademark Reg. U.S. Pat. Off. and in Other Countries, Marca Registrada, Hecho en U.S.A.
HarperCollins® is a registered trademark of HarperCollins Publishers.

Printed in the U.S.A.

10 9 8 7 6 5 4 3 2 1

This book is dedicated to the one who told me
to start writing and never lets me stop.

Contents

Sundays

I don't really love sex. I mean, I do. I love the thrusting, raw, powerful energy that two people create when they're really losing themselves in a moment, driven toward one single purpose of pure visceral satisfaction. Even more than that, though, I love the electric, tangible, skin-tingling energy that two people create when they want to fuck more than anything—but can't.

You can't argue with me here—the one touch you get as your coveted, yet completely unattainable, object of lust brushes her hand over your thigh while reaching past you to get her pen is unquestionably ten times louder than the slap of your wife's hand on your ass while you're pounding your cock into her a million times a minute.

Oh, how I craved that hand-over-thigh, that two-second brush of fingers against neck while exchanging a platonic hug good-bye—so vivid you wonder for hours afterward if it lasted for two seconds or five, and what that three-second difference could imply.

I lived for knowing that, while pressed four to the backseat, squeezed against the door in just such a way that my hand had to rest innocently on my neighbor's leg, I could use every bump, every turn, to let my hand even more innocently slide up the leg, stealing moments to slip down the thigh, perhaps a bit too close—but the car was moving, we were packed in, I was even carrying on a conversation at the time, it could not have been intentional—but just close enough to run my hand down where the jeans were hot, grinning inwardly every time, knowing the jeans were hotter and the fit a bit tighter as a result, my poor neighbor struggling to keep his face calm while the four of us bounced along to our destination.

Did I want to fuck him? Absolutely not. I just needed my fix, like any junkie, and I took it where I could get it. I somehow always managed to be the first one without a chair—don't mind me, I'll just sit on someone's lap—knowing that my skirt was short and my underwear virtually nonexistent, and that, once seated, my skirt would rise up enough to expose bare thighs that he couldn't help but touch whenever reaching for his drink. I made sure he couldn't help it by spreading my legs just the right amount to make sure I created a tight traffic situation when his hands had to get by. I sat on the lap and made sure, every time I had to turn left or right—which happened just often enough—to swivel my hips and press while turning, each time feeling his cock getting a bit harder and just a bit more uncomfortable between the seams of his jeans.

I wasn't a tease—I just lived for the thrill, the energy, the hot, tingling touches of unfulfilled, frustrated desire.

And then I hit a snag—I fell in love with Peter.

At first, it was great. I was a junkie who had just discovered I could make my drug out of water. The thrill was everywhere. I reveled in its excess and accessibility. There is nothing like new romance to make energy out of nothing—I took cabs to meet him rather than walk the extra blocks when I just couldn't wait a minute longer. We squeezed our schedules into silly putty, bending everything around when we could meet—to kiss, to touch, to fuck. We never made it through a single movie. We couldn't sit in the same room without having to wrap ourselves around each other. Every party ended up with us locked in the bathroom, clothes on the floor, figuring out yet another way to fuck against the sink. Every dinner ended with us sitting next to each other, ignoring our food, busy trying covertly to slip hands inside pants and up shirts.

Like all young romance, though, it got old. We moved in together, and the electricity started to fade, competing with dog walks and alarm clocks, errand running and laundry. Suddenly, my most intimate interaction with the sink was cleaning it. I couldn't even remember the last time Peter pushed me to the floor and fucked me before I'd even taken off my coat—and now that I'd known what fucking with Peter could be like, I knew there was no way I could go back to feeling satisfied by stolen thigh-strokes or an extra three seconds of fingers on neck. I needed that energy back with Peter, or I'd waste away.

One afternoon, I figured how to do it. I had lain down to take a nap, when Peter decided to come and sleep beside me. He didn't usually take naps, but we'd both been up late the night before, and I guess he decided to try it. By the time he'd gotten into bed, I was already half-asleep. He curled up against me, his boxer shorts against my underwear, his bare chest against my T-shirt, his arm around my waist, while we tried to fall asleep. I was practically there already, so his warmth just helped me drift off. However, not a nap taker by nature, and still awake, Peter did not have as easy a time.

While I tried to sleep, I could feel his cock start to harden between my legs. He shifted away from me, not wanting to disturb me, but, almost unconsciously, my hips followed his, and I slid my ass back into the curve of his pelvis. His cock was officially hard, and it began to press between my legs. I let myself hang there, still half-asleep, feeling the delicious sensation of being desired, knowing that he wanted to take a nap but that his cock had a mind of its own. I could tell that his cock had slipped through the opening in his boxer shorts, and I could feel his skin against my thigh. I shifted imperceptibly, still feigning sleep, just enough to allow his cock to slide between my legs.

While I pretended to lie innocently beside him, I could feel his blood rushing to his cock as it pressed against the crotch of my underwear. I languorously stretched my right leg back, slipping it between his legs, pinning his cock even harder between my thighs, shifting my hip enough to press his cock sharply into my underwear against the wetness that was seeping out of my pussy. All this, of course, while I dozed peacefully.

Peter was beside himself. He couldn't move, or at least, couldn't bring himself to move, since the sensation felt so good, but, at the same time, it was driving him crazy. He thought I was sound asleep, and he knew how much I hated being awakened from my precious naps, so there he was, desperate to fuck, desperate to start moving against me, and unable to do anything but try to calm himself down mentally in order to fall asleep—a task that, at this point, was virtually impossible.

I grinned to myself, loving it. I knew he could feel my wetness, which was drenching my underwear, the tip of his cock pressed against me, prevented from attaining actual contact by a thin bit of satiny fabric. His hand was still draped around my waist, and I could tell, by the little movements he did allow himself to make, running his fingers in subtle circles across my stomach and hips, that only an impressive amount of respect for my sleep and stubborn self-discipline was preventing him from rolling me over, pulling down my underwear, and fucking me.

I lay there, every inch of my flesh feeling the hardening of his cock, the stroking of his fingers, the pressure of his thigh, the heat of his breath. It was killing him. As desperation began to get the best of him, the movements of his hand grew more pronounced, pressing into my flesh, the circles gradually widening to include my thighs, my hips, my waist, my breasts. His breathing grew heavier as the circles grew larger, and the pressure grew stronger. If there had been any distance between his hips and mine, it was now gone—his cock pressing deeper into my underwear, his hips starting to shove impatiently at mine.

I waited just long enough until his mind had officially given up on sleeping and had become fully consumed by the prospect of sex—feeling the beginnings of steady thrusting pressing my underwear to the side, the tip of his cock searching its way into my pussy—waiting just long enough for the anticipation to reach its maximum peak before action would take over, before languorously stretching myself out with a gesture, oh-so-innocently allowing his cock a split-second entry into the wet darkness of my insides before rolling over away from him with a sigh.

"I'm sleeping," I murmured, under my breath, as I buried my head in the pillow, keeping any satisfaction out of my voice as I feigned tired annoyance.

What could he say? I had announced my nap intention, I had done nothing to encourage his advances (or so he thought), and I had been sleeping when he got into bed (or so he thought). He had no cause for argument. A good guy, a nice guy, a solid guy, Peter let out the tiniest of sighs, rolled himself over away from me, and left the bedroom, leaving me alone, tense and excited, my brain working a mile a minute.

No longer needing to pretend, I stretched myself out under the covers and stared at the ceiling. Those few minutes of sexual frustration brought back the highlights of my earlier days. Except for the rare lucky moment, I'd given up on ever feeling that way again while I was with Peter, but now, but now I was onto something. I could keep my wonderful relationship and still get back that delicious thrill I'd really started to miss. I knew exactly what had to be done.

Satisfied with my realizations, I curled back up and went to sleep.

What was the realization? Sex could only happen on Sundays. Kissing and groping could happen any day, but proper satisfaction could only come once a week. It was perfect. The ultimate diet plan. It didn't matter how much he wanted it, or how wet I got between the legs, rules were rules, and we had to wait. It would be better that way.

I got to play the games I wanted during the week. I got to feel Peter's lust, his hard, unsatisfied cock forced to sleep next to me six nights a week, I got to look at his warm sweet puppy-dog eyes dazed with desire, and I got to leave my fingers on his neck for three extra seconds, knowing how that translated to pressure inside his jeans. Then, Sunday—who had time for brunch? Sometimes, when we both got really hot and hard and wet after a particularly satisfying Saturday night, we let Sundays start at midnight. Of course, then we'd stay up until four, which just meant we'd spend all the next day in bed.

It really was the perfect arrangement.

The first week of the plan, everything went smoothly, until Friday night—although, in my opinion, Friday night was where it got good. Peter and I had gone out to dinner with some friends. After five days of abstinence, we were back to pawing each other like fresh loves. Our friends kept being polite and trying to pretend they didn't notice, but we were virtually clawing at each other under the table. They just sighed when I got up to go to the bathroom a minute after Peter left to make a phone call—they'd seen all this before, and, just like our old routine, I slid into the stall as Peter slipped in right behind me.

The sink and I were back to being friends, the only difference being that the only thing pressed inside me was Peter's hand, and, even though I grabbed his cock from outside his boxer shorts, no one came—we weren't allowed to. The only act accomplished was a noticeable increase in facial flush.

Hair mussed, cheeks pink, we returned to our table, wetness leaking between my legs, Peter walking carefully to conceal his hard cock as it pressed into the seam of his pants. Getting through the rest of the meal was an exercise in discipline— trying to maintain composure, trying to maintain conversation, trying to maintain relaxed faces while our fingers frantically crept under each other's shirts, sneaking behind waistbands and inside pockets, groping every inch of available (and unavailable) flesh.

By the time dessert arrived, both Peter and I were hot, hard, and unable to sit still—yet somehow I managed to keep smiling, talking, and acting as though I had no idea my nipples were fiercely rigid against my bra or that I'd already managed to stain the cushion of my chair. I had no idea at all as I ordered the cherry pie.

When the waiter placed it in front of me, I could barely look at it—the crust brown and flaky, completely unable to conceal the cherries as they oozed out the sides, shimmering, wet, and glossy, red, vibrant, and warm. At first I stared, but the sensation was too intense, I felt as though the cherries themselves were seeping out of me. While the conversation pattered on, my hand, casually resting between my legs under the table, slowly began reaching up my skirt. I playfully flicked my finger back and forth against my pussy, feeling how wet it was, before sliding my finger in up to my third knuckle. I left it there for a few seconds, my chest clenched, my lungs on pause, my breath somewhere in my throat. Then, with a slow and subtle sigh, I pulled it out. I brought my hand back up to the table and looked at my finger, wet and glistening. No one was paying any attention.

I looked at Peter. "Do you want to taste mine? It's very good."

He looked up, startled, his mind clearly somewhere between my legs. My finger plunged into the pie as Peter opened his mouth, probably to remind me that he didn't like cherry pie.

Before he could get a word out, I slid my finger into his mouth, running it over his tongue while he closed his lips around me. I dragged it out slowly, staring him straight in the eyes, every last molecule of wetness left behind in his mouth. I could tell the second the cherries gave way to the tart taste of my insides.

"It's very good, you're right," Peter said, as we tried to hide our grins.

Our friends looked at us, knowing that they were missing a joke but still having no idea what, exactly, had just transpired. All they could do was watch my finger, now clean of cherry pie and crumbs, as it reached for my fork.

By the time dessert had been eaten, check paid, coats zipped, good-byes exchanged, and cabs hailed, the sexual frustration had become almost unmanageable. The two of us tumbled into the cab, already starting to grab each other before we were fully seated, knowing we couldn't have sex, that we weren't going to have sex, that we still had one more day before either of us would feel satisfied—and knowing that was going to drive us crazy.

I leaned back in the cab, feeling my teeth start to grind together. Trying to stop, I dug my nails into the dark leather of the seat, attempting to transfer my tension into the plush padding of the cab. Peter's arm around me, he squeezed tightly on my shoulder as both of us tried to pull ourselves together. I took a couple of deep breaths, reminding myself to enjoy the moment, to revel in the energy, trying to focus on how great Sunday would feel.

That lasted all of thirty seconds before the makeout began.

We both wanted to explode—his cock hardening, trying to force through his pants, his hand between my legs, gripping my pussy as though he wanted to pull it from me. I slid my hand under his coat and beneath his shirt, running my fingers down his back, my nails leaving trails along his skin. I could feel him pinching my pussy lips through my underwear. It hurt, but when he let go, all I wanted was his hand back. I knew I was on the verge of coming, but I couldn't help myself, I couldn't slow it down. I wanted more, and I didn't want to wait.

I grabbed hold of his crotch, squeezing and pushing back harshly, feeling every cell in the skin on his cock becoming alive, tingling when I let go, craving my grip. I shoved myself at him, pushing my hips back in the direction of his hand.

"What are you doing?" he whispered fiercely, barely able to get the words out.

I didn't even respond, I just unzipped his pants and slid my hand inside. He tried feebly to push my hand away but quickly gave up, leaning back in the seat, panting, as my hand starting rubbing rapidly. Watching the look on his face, I suddenly realized what I was doing. I was breaking my rule, and we hadn't even made it a week. I pulled my hand back and closed up my coat. Every girl knows how important it is to follow the rules.

Peter sat up and looked at me, eyes completely glazed, cock sticking out of his shorts.

"You're right," I said, clinically and calmly. "We can't do any more."

He leaned over and tried to slip his hand through the gap between the buttons of my coat, rubbing himself against my thigh, but I blocked him and shook my head. I looked at his cock, still rigid, and smiled to myself. I had forgotten how much fun this part could be.

The best part, of course, was Saturday night. Peter and I had both agreed that Sunday would officially begin at 12:01, and we were counting down the minutes. The evening started with a movie, a large, loud action feature that blitzed and bombed its way across the screen, sensational enough to provide a distracting plot, but not so engrossing that we minded missing large bits of dialogue while sending hands inside shirts and tongues inside mouths.

Knowing our level of frustration and our frequently inappropriate behavior, we found seats in the back of the theater, in the far corner, where the usual Saturday night crowd wouldn't notice if my skirt got hiked up to my waist or if Peter's pants got unzipped. Of course, both happened before the previews had finished.

Our popcorn sat neglected as Peter's hands gently, and then increasingly firmly, rubbed my breasts. I leaned back in the seat, oblivious to the Dolby Surround Sound, feeling the straight line of electricity run from my chest to my pussy and down my legs. Peter, sensing my growing heat, gently pushed my shirt up, pulled my bra down, and slipped his tongue around my nipple.

Oh God, I thought to myself, tensing my thighs, pointing my

toes, and slipping even farther into the seat. I was already starting to stain my pants, the leaking seeping rapidly through the lips of my pussy and into my underwear. Peter ran his hand down my waist, across my stomach, and underneath my waistband, effortlessly popping open the snap as he slid his way down between my legs.

As much as I knew this would make the rest of the movie interminable, I arched toward him, pressing my crotch against his hand, desperate to experience the satisfaction of his fingers against my pussy, the few moments of pleasure I would feel before they were replaced with all-consuming frustration. I got about three seconds before I couldn't even see straight. I wanted his fingers inside me. I felt the emptiness consume me, and I couldn't wait a second longer—I pulled my pants down to my knees, tugged my underwear to one side.

"Please," I whispered.

With the hint of a smile, Peter looked up and, without taking his eyes off my face, pressed one, then two of his fingers inside me. I couldn't help it, I moaned, curving my hips down around his hand. No one seemed to notice, engrossed as they were by the audio assault of the feature. Ever so slowly, Peter began to slide his fingers in and out. I made an attempt to reach for his pants but, just as my fingers brushed the edge of his zipper, Peter pushed his fingers deep into me, and my hand fell limply by my side.

The fingers slipped out, hesitating for a split second, near my clitoris, and then reached their way back in, pressing against my

G-spot before slipping back out. My head leaning back against the edge of my seat, my eyes closed, little orbs of white light dancing through my head, my body managing to be both perfectly taut and completely useless at the same time, every cell in my body swinging up and down to Peter's perfect rhythm.

As the rhythm grew faster, the white lights picked up speed, and my fingers clenched my seat. Peter moved his fingers out with professional efficiency, and I lay back, praying for more, more, more. Every part of me was primed and ready and aching, a delicious tingling running from head to toe, stopping to linger between my legs. Peter slid his other hand up my stomach and reached for my nipple. Pinching it lightly, he sent me falling into a tunnel of white lights, a quiet roar in my ears.

Just as everything began to sync up—the lights, the roar, the tingling, the fingers—Peter stopped, his index finger gently pressed against my G-spot. I froze—lights on pause, roar on mute—and waited, everything on hold. Then, with the careful precision of a surgeon or a sadist, Peter slid his fingers out, licked them, and stared calmly at me.

I wanted to scream.

I took a deep breath, a very deep breath, and waited for everything to return to order. Once I had managed to get hold of my senses, recovering from the precipice Peter had coaxed me toward, I breathed again, pretending all the while to be riveted by our motion picture. Damn the bastard.

I stared straight ahead, watching the barrel-chested pinup

star race down a wet alleyway, both guns blaring, feeling Peter's eyes on me. I ignored him. I would have my revenge. I waited until the alley scene was over, until after the pinup had wrestled the leather-clad bad guy to the ground and cuffed him, until after the fast-paced police station booking and the lonely drink at the bar while we sympathize with our troubled star, until after the obligatory sex scene with the rescued prostitute. Only after all those scenes had passed, during which I stared straight ahead, ate my popcorn, and acted as though nothing untoward was running through my brain, only then did I very slowly reach my arm through Peter's. I reached my arm through his and rested it, casually, on his thigh.

Peter glanced over at me, but I was too busy staring straight ahead to make eye contact.

I waited another scene—this one full of some inconsequential car chase—until I made my move. My hand crept down Peter's thigh, making its way between his legs, then paused, for an instant, just long enough to make Peter wonder if I'd keep moving, then fingers found cock. As I suspected, it was already hard and pressing against the seam of his pants. I decided to increase the pressure. I began to rub.

Peter's breath grew louder and faster as my hand moved harder and faster. Fingers on either side of his cock, running along the edge of it, palm of my hand pressing down on the shaft, I rubbed hand against corduroy, Peter's cock becoming more and more pronounced against the ridges of the soft fabric.

Just when I thought his cock might burst through his pants, when Peter's breathing couldn't get any faster, I reached over, grabbed hold of his zipper, and pulled down. As Peter sighed with pleasure, matched only by the relief of release, his cock sprang out of his pants, and I ran my mouth around it.

Gently moving my mouth up and down as Peter stretched back in the seat, I gave him about two minutes of warm, wet satisfaction before sitting up, wiping my mouth, and grabbing a handful of popcorn—back to the feature presentation.

Peter lay back in his seat for a little while longer, not moving, not opening his eyes, just breathing steadily. I ignored him—or, actually, I pretended to ignore him while carefully noticing his every move. After his breath returned to normal, Peter sat up, zipped himself back together, and leaned over to give me a kiss on the cheek before asking for more popcorn.

We were the perfect pair.

By the time the movie finished, we were sitting together like any respectable middle-aged couple, popcorn exhausted, arms interlocked, calmly witnessing the adventures of our pinup and his sexy starlet. We slowly got up as the closing credits concluded, donned our coats, and filed out with the rest of our respectable Saturday night theater crowd.

We made our way to the street and stood there for a second, letting everyone else head toward their next destination. We stood there and looked at our watches. It was eleven-thirty. Like all the other middle-aged couples, it was time for us to go home.

The cab couldn't drive fast enough. The lights, the traffic, the elevator—nothing moved at the speed we wanted. We made it home in record time, but it still felt too long. We burst into our apartment, a mess of shedding coats and dropping bags, losing mittens and discarding hats—and we were naked, on the bed, staring at each other.

I laughed. It seemed too good to be true. It was that moment, when it's finally Christmas and all your gifts are lined up in front of you, waiting to be ravaged. In that instant, you own the world, everything is possible, anything you want could be neatly wrapped in paper in front of you, and you savor it, like the most perfect delicious chocolate mousse.

And then, like Christmas, when you've sat and looked and savored for just the right amount of time, you absolutely can't stand it anymore and you dig right in, and you rip and you tear and you toss and you stare, you throw and you shake and you push and you shove, until there's nowhere to go, and you've plundered it all.

That's exactly what it was like—the bliss, the ecstasy, the wild, rapid frenzy. The two of us looked at each other for that perfect moment, hints of grins tugging at our lips, and then we dove—I wrapped my arms around his neck and pulled him to me, as he wrapped his arms around my waist and dragged me to him, and I pushed my tongue into his mouth as his cock slid into my pussy, and we pressed ourselves against each other until there wasn't an inch of air to spare, and it was thigh against thigh, stomach against stomach, chest against chest, and it was sweaty and raw, and my legs went around his waist, and my ankles intertwined behind his back, and he grabbed my lower back and tugged me tighter, and he went in as I pushed out, and our hips melded into a perfect complementary shape, fused by sweat and desire. His cock couldn't have been farther inside me, but still my hips arched higher, my knees clenched tighter, my thighs pressed harder, and he thrust and thrust, delicious pleasure running through every ounce of my being, flooding my insides from my intertwined ankles to the hair he was pulling, and the white lights started blinking.

Oh God, I wanted more.

I started to pull him deeper into me, running my nails down his back, but Peter took my legs and placed them down on the bed. He reached his hands underneath the small of my back and pushed me away from him, slipping himself out in the process. With one hand, he took first one arm, then the other, lifting them over my head and placing them down on the pillow above me. Holding them in place with his left hand, he took his right hand and ran his index finger from my forehead, lingering slightly on my lips, dipping momentarily into my mouth, before continuing slowly down my neck, between my breasts, across my chest, resting interminably on my stomach before making his way between my legs and into the deep wetness of my pussy.

Teasing me, tormenting me, he ran his fingers along the outside of my pussy and around my clitoris, just enough pressure to send the blood rushing to the surface but not enough to bring me any kind of release. I moaned, pleading with him to go harder. He just smiled and continued his dancing, left hand still pressing my wrists against the pillow. His finger flitted about, just ever so barely dipping inside before skirting the edges of everything. When I literally couldn't stand it anymore, when my hips were twisting every which way in an attempt to somehow trap his hand and suck it in, Peter complied and sent several fingers inward. Bliss.

I lay back, legs spread wide, wrists willingly inactive, and let him do his work. Fingers went in, deep, curling up just enough to send shivers to my G-spot and blood to my clitoris. My eyes closed, I let the sensation from that one small part of my body consume the rest of me. Harder, faster, he pressed in and out, then—just when I thought I couldn't be wetter—he shoved his fingers inside and left them there, taking his thumb to my clitoris in small, perfect circles. That was all it took. I could feel an orgasm building, and I still couldn't move. It was too perfect. I lay there, feeling each little pore fill up with sensation—the tingling all-consuming.

Just when I was on the edge of coming, when every cell had grown tight with tension and desire, when my hips were thrust against his fingers, when my clitoris almost pained me as it ached for every glancing touch of his circling thumb, Peter stopped, reading my signals for what they were, and withdrew his hand. He ran his wet fingers back up my body, forming damp rings around my nipples and across my chest, before slipping them into my mouth. I licked them, tasting myself, knowing that the gentle pressure of my tongue was sending similar jolts of electricity down Peter's arm. Sucking and licking, I felt the prodding of his cock grow harder and more insistent between my legs. Keeping his fingers in my mouth, I arched my back just enough to let his cock reach the edge of my pussy, his precum mingling with my dripping wetness.

The second his skin touched my skin, he froze and let out a slow breath. Taking that as all the encouragement I needed, I shoved my hips at him, and he shoved his hips at me—again and again and again, deeper and harder and faster and harder and deeper and faster—until, in a moment of rush and heat, we both came, and the light show exploded.

We collapsed, completely entangled, entirely spent. The bed was drenched, and so were we. I lay back, feeling Peter still inside me, my arms and knees and thighs holding him close, our breathing gradually slowing down.

The only thing more perfect was the knowledge that we still had twenty-three more hours left.

Sivan

I can't remember the first time I saw her. It might have
been when she was on the street corner, waiting for us to
pick her up, but then I didn't know who she was, or that
it was us she was waiting for, so I didn't pay much attention until the car had stopped, the door had opened, and
she got in. I still didn't pay much attention because I
was sitting in front, and she got in the back, and I hate
riding with my head turned around because it makes me
feel sick, so I just sort of gave her a quick introductory
smile and spoke to her while facing toward the front
windshield. I remember noticing how skinny she was
and how elegant she looked in a sweater that hung off
her shoulder in fabric so sheer it was clearly never intended to provide any kind of warmth. And then there
was maybe a vague recollection of a pleasing face with

21

brown hair sort of framing it, but that's really it. I just noticed her voice and her laugh while we drove, and I watched the traffic and the sky.

Which means, I guess, that the first time I really saw her was when we got out of the car. Actually, no, that's not true. When we got out of the car and walked through the parking lot to the bar, I still wasn't paying much attention. I was talking to my friend, lost in thought, doing whatever one does when not really doing anything, negotiating my way in high heels through the stones of the courtyard, until we sat down, and I somehow ended up facing her across the small table. I was facing her while my friend went to the bathroom, then I noticed. That's when I first really saw her.

Not that I remember what I saw first. No, wait, I do—it was the line of her neck as it curved down to her shoulder. So delicate, so fragile, so smooth, that I marveled biology could craft something like that, DNA and not an artist. Then I got overwhelmed. I saw her eyes, her teeth, her hair, her skin, her legs, her waist, her wrists, her fingers, her legs, and it was just this overload of deliciousness, and I wanted to eat her and take her home and taste that line of her neck—so I ordered a drink and told her about Berlin just to clear the air.

There was no point. A girl like that had to be straight.

I couldn't help noticing, even though I knew it wasn't worth my time, how she laughed, how she held her glass, and how her skinny, graceful arms moved in a way that might make Baryshnikov jealous.

I had another drink and tried to focus on the sunset.

I actually managed to forget about her. Well, not forget about her entirely, but to think about other things and not what she might be doing or thinking or feeling. Life actually proceeded in a relatively normal fashion—normal meaning without emotional entanglements, complications, or obsessions—until I ended up at her house, next to her on the couch, in front of a movie.

I'd called Roberta earlier to see if she wanted to do something, and she had just picked out two movies and was on her way to Sivan's for a night on the couch. Did I want to come? Well, of course, that was an easy question.

From the second we got to her house, when Sivan offered me something in the kitchen (water? juice?) and asked if I ate popcorn, I knew I didn't want to be anywhere else.

The kitchen wasn't so big, but I didn't see anything else in it. I kind of remember Roberta at the table out of the corner of my eye, rolling a cigarette, but I really just saw Sivan moving. It was like watching one of those stop-action flipbooks, where sometimes the movements feel fluid and smooth, and other times they freeze into little sequences—the way she moved her wrist, for instance, when opening the bottle of water. The way she ripped open the cardboard package of microwave popcorn. The way she laughed when I said something that, for once, wasn't insipid but almost funny. The way she leaned against the corner and the way the line of her shirt ran down her chest, exposing the perfect triangle of skin.

At some point, we left the kitchen, carrying the bowls and the water and the glasses, and set up camp on the couch. With perfect plot development, she sat on my left, Roberta on my right, but I knew it didn't matter where I sat, or where she sat, or how much energy might have been flowing between the two of us. I knew I'd never touch her, at least not with the movie playing and Roberta on my right, and I knew she'd never touch me, it didn't matter the timing or the circumstance. I knew she was dating some boy named Mick, some boy that Roberta had told me about, in response to some overly casual questions intended to gather as much information in as subtle a fashion.

Mick worked the bar at the same restaurant where Sivan waitressed. He was six years older than her, three years out of the army. He drove a motorcycle and lived in the south part of town. He was also an aspiring photographer and always seemed to be surrounded by tall seventeen-year-old models with long blond hair and willowy figures. Of course, Sivan was completely different from those girls, which is why the relationship might or might not be work depending on the given day and the given opinion.

Sivan wasn't tall. Her hair wasn't blond. She was definitely willowy, but on that small a frame, it didn't create a willowy impression. It created a precious, fragile, exquisite impression, where you marveled at the tiny precision of her wrists, the sophistication of her fingers, the miniature size of her waist. It made you want to hold her, protect her, and just look at her.

Her hair was brown, soft, short, layered. I never really noticed it too much because it was so close to her face, which captivated most of my attention. Like with most things that capture our heart, or our obsessions, my affection wasn't precise. It wasn't because of the color of her eyes or their distance from each other or the shape of her nose or the size of her lips—when I closed my eyes, I couldn't even see any of those details anyway. I just saw a vague impression of elegance and warmth and the whiteness of her teeth in a mouth I wanted to taste and eyes I wanted to stare at.

I focused on the movie, though, because I knew about Mick, and I knew she didn't like girls, and the last thing I wanted was a broken heart. Every lesbian knows straight girls are a recipe for disaster.

But that didn't stop me from following her back into the kitchen after the movie, it didn't stop me from asking what she was doing the next day, and it didn't stop me from inviting myself over.

Even though I kept telling myself it wasn't a date, I still felt that predate nervousness, with the sweaty palms and the anxious stomach churning and the constant fidgeting of the hair. I had no idea what she wanted, or what I should expect.

What I didn't expect was her boyfriend.

"Hey there. Come on in." He grinned at me as he stood beside the open door. "Can I get you something to drink?"

I blinked. This was not according to plan.

"Just a juice or something. Is Sivan around?"

"Yeah, she's in the kitchen. Go on in."

I made my way to the kitchen, Mick right behind me. What was he doing here? What was I doing here?

"Hey, darling, hello. How's it going?" Her perfect Cindy Crawford grin slid across her perfect Michelangelo face, and the predate nervousness returned, Mick's testosterone notwithstanding.

I stammered an inconsequential reply and gratefully took my juice from Mick, so at least one of my hands would have a purpose while the other one got shoved out of the way into my pocket.

"Are you sure you wouldn't like a glass of wine with that?" Sivan asked, leaning over and smiling at me.

"A glass of wine would be lovely," I said gratefully.

"Perfect! There's a bottle on the balcony. I figured we could go sit out there, the weather's so nice today."

I made my way out to the balcony, trailing after Sivan and Mick.

"Come sit next to me," she purred, patting the small amount of space next to her on the balcony's miniscule couch. "Mick, why don't you sit over there and let the girls have some time together . . . ?" She gestured across to the facing chair.

Mick grinned. "Two girls together? I'll watch that any day."

I wanted to punch him, or at least ask him to please leave, but I restrained myself, too distracted by the sensation of Sivan's thigh against mine, her arm across my neck and shoulders, wondering if I could actually feel the soft hairs along her skin and her breath on my neck, or if that was just my imagination.

"Oh, come on, Mick. Do you have to be so predictable?" Sivan laughed. "If we were getting it on together, you think you'd be allowed to watch?" She laughed again (nervously, maybe?) and ran her hand down my arm in a gesture of mock flirtation.

"What do you say? Should we let him watch?" She squeezed my upper arm.

My head was spinning. What was going on here?

Sivan and Mick just laughed. I laughed, too, to keep up.

"Of course, I wouldn't do anything. I'd just watch. It would be all about the two of you. I wouldn't do anything or anything. You'd barely even notice I was there."

"Right, Mick, sure. You'd barely do anything."

More laughter. More head spinning. Was it the wine?

Somehow the conversation shifted. Somehow we got to music and movies and beer and I almost forgot about the jokes—until Mick ran out to get some beer.

"Don't do anything without me, now, you girls hear?"

"Like what, Mick? Like what? Like this?" Sivan slipped her hand down to the inside of my right thigh and laughed. "You mean like this? You mean like this?"

27

She was officially stroking the inside of my right thigh. She was stroking my thigh. How much wine had she had to drink? I tried to remember how many glasses she'd refilled. I tried to remember if there was another bottle lying around. I tried to think about anything else other than the fact that her hand was still holding on to my right thigh, even while she kissed Mick goodbye. Especially while she kissed Mick good-bye. She kissed him, and her fingers tightened, I was sure they tightened, while his tongue was in her mouth. His tongue was in her mouth, and her hand was still on my damn thigh.

Then he left, and we were alone. Together.

"Do you, um, want some water or something? I was going to get some juice or, you know, something nonalcoholic to drink." I laughed nervously, standing up quickly, letting her hand fall back on her thigh.

I stood in front of her, in front of her reclining on the couch, her legs a little spread apart . . . I shook my head. I had to get my head out of the gutter. This was Sivan, nice straight girl with nice straight boyfriend, and she'd just had a little to drink and I was misreading all her signals because all I wanted was to see her naked on her bed with my fingers inside her. I was getting all the signals crossed because I couldn't stop thinking about the taste of her skin and her sweat, and I needed, instead, to think about the taste of the grapefruit juice I was about to have.

"I. Don't. Want. Any. Juice." Her tone was serious. Each word slow and precise.

She stared at me. She stared at me, and I started feeling really, really nervous.

"I don't want any juice."

This time she grinned, and I grinned hesitantly back at her.

"Why don't you sit back down?"

"Oh, yeah, I will, uh, just let me get some juice."

I turned around. She grabbed my belt and pulled me back onto the couch. Actually, she pulled me back onto the couch on top of her.

"Sit back down." She laughed, as I tried to get myself off her. "Can't the juice wait?"

I had no idea what to say.

"Can't you kiss me first?"

"What? You, you, you—what?"

"Kiss me."

She tugged me, via my shirt, toward her, and pressed her mouth against mine. The sweetness of the wine mixed with the sweetness of her lips—I probably would have been more coherent if I'd actually blacked out. It was as though there was a direct line of energy running from between her legs to between mine, while the pulsing beats throbbed through my toes, and I wanted to push myself into her and herself into me to somehow try to appease the hunger pains. Just being able to smell her skin, to feel her coolness against me, her flesh so close to mine, knowing that I could run my tongue over any part and taste her, that I could take my teeth to any part of her and bite her, was almost more information, more opportunity, than I could handle.

I was mesmerized, lost somewhere in the mix of taste and sensation, her mouth against mine, her tongue in mine, mine in hers, her hand against my back, then her hand against my waist and her hand under my shirt, all the while too aware of the fact that this could end at any moment—and it was just this chaotic mess where nothing made sense, and everything felt right, and I was there and I wasn't, and it was brilliant and confusing, and there was more energy, more electricity, more power and lust and desire, and it was her and me and her taste and mine and her lips and cheekbones and her neck and her wrists, and everything was like a van Gogh painting where the parts fit together, and it was a whole and it wasn't a whole at the same time. There was no perspective, and nothing was right or normal, and my insides ran out somewhere between my legs and every part of my body was between her legs, and I wanted to eat it all and taste it all and fill myself up with her and fill her up with me.

Then her fingers slipped between my legs and, before I could wonder how much practice a straight girl could have had, I knew she had done enough. It was all I could do to curve myself against her hand, to press my hips down and my chest out, to feel her fingers pressing deep inside, against those perfect places that somehow she found as though I'd helped her find the way. I shifted slowly, rhythmically, back and forth, against her hand, feeling the waves of sensation, my eyes closed, my body lost in a world where my mind had stopped knowing how to operate—

—until she leaned over and ran her tongue lightly over the edges of my nipples, and I snapped awake with the realization that I had to devour her. I pushed her down, pushed her outside of me, against the couch, and I pushed myself inside her. I pushed my fingers between her legs, my tongue in her mouth, my left hand against her breasts, and I tried to get my fill of her sweet, hot, wetness.

And then I heard the door open and shut, and Mick's footsteps were coming toward us. Somehow I retrieved my hand and somehow her hand was no longer under my shirt, and somehow we weren't on top of each other anymore but just next to each other and everything look organized again—except for my insides, which were still running on their own private roller coaster.

"Hey girls. Didn't do anything I wouldn't have, right?"

"No, Mick, not at all." Sivan smiled. "Not without you watching."

I squirmed, both mentally and physically. My insides were leaking all over my underwear, and I wondered if I was staining the couch. I could feel my clit throbbing, and I wanted more, more, more. Who was this guy and why was he back? Why was he back, and why wouldn't he leave?

I watched Sivan talk to him, I watched her laugh, her hand on his arm, kissing his cheek, I watched it all, and I wondered how she did it. She was normal, she was cool, she was acting fucking straight. She was acting like her fingers hadn't just been inside me.

She was acting as though she wasn't being tormented with sexual frustration, by the sensation of an orgasm just on the edge of the horizon, but I could feel that orgasm, and I wanted it—now.

"Mick? Do you mind . . . ?"

He turned to look at me, his oafish grin and his puppy-dog brown eyes causing even me to find him slightly endearing despite the fact that he was the last thing I wanted in that room.

"What's up?"

"I'm totally out of cigarettes. I don't suppose you have any?" (I knew he didn't. I'd seen him finish his pack earlier.)

"Yeah, sure, of course."

He reached into his pockets as my stomach dropped.

"Uh—wait." He searched a bit. "Shit, no, I finished 'em." He paused. "Don't worry, I've got to get more, anyway. I'll be back in a sec."

With that, with a turn and a wink at Sivan, he was gone. He was gone, and we were alone. It really was that easy.

I turned to her and pushed her up against the wall. I watched her blue eyes close. My fingers deep inside her, her wetness, her warmth, the soft smoothness of her insides, I pushed and pushed. I wanted her damn orgasm more than I wanted my own. I wanted to feel her melt against me. I wanted to feel her throb on my fingers.

It didn't take twenty seconds. She was mine. All over me, all over my hands, all over my fingers, all over my mouth and my lips. And then she was in me, her fingers shoved up inside, her thumb against my clit, her other fingers somewhere I couldn't even explain because I couldn't tell where they were touching me, I just knew I could barely stand the sensation—the power, her force, the electricity, and I was strong against her hand, and I was weak against her hand, and she went in and out as I sighed and breathed and shoved against her and fell against the wall, and then I came, melting against her, and I was wet against her—

And then I heard Mick coming back up the stairs.

"Later, honey," she said, winking at me, as she ran her fingers over her hair and pulled her skirt back down. "Later. We'll do it again."

And then she kissed me, fast, as the door opened.

At Work

He pushed me up against the stairwell wall. I didn't have time to worry if anyone might be around—I was too busy reeling from the pressure of his body, from the heat between his legs and the heat between mine.

"Oh God, I've been wanting to do this all day," he panted, as his hand shoved its way past my waistband, behind my underwear, down to my crotch.

Matt angled his fingers against the tight fabric of my pants, pressing them inside me as much as he could, sliding in and out, an inch or two inside me. I shoved my hips against his hand, trying to get him in deeper. Sensing my urgency and feeding it with his own, he pushed harder and harder until, with a small clang, my button fell to the floor, and my pants split open.

"Oh shit," he said, his hand slipping out as he turned to look for the button.

"Forget it," I replied, grabbing his waist with my arms and pulling him back to me, my hands and my hips combining efforts to fill myself up with his fingers. I'd felt empty all day, and I wasn't anywhere near satisfied.

The thrusting of his hands began to be mirrored by the thrusting of his hips, reminding me to shove my hand between our two bodies. Despite the miniscule amount of space between his hips and mine, it was easy to find what I was looking for—his cock was practically bucking against his pants, huge, engorged, and hot. I grabbed it and held it, feeling its frustrated energy send sparks up my arm, while he kept making my pussy wetter and wetter, the liquid seeping out onto his fingers and my pants.

I started to rub, my fingers tightening along the edges of his shaft, pressing in, as I moved slowly up and down along its length, reveling in the perfect way my hand cupped around it. He moaned and pushed against me even harder, pressing me flat against the wall. I kept rubbing, picking up speed and pressure, while his fingers gradually slowed their pace inside me, until they were just pressed inside, the only movement stemming from shoving my hips against them.

"Oh God, I'm going to come," he moaned.

"That's fine," I replied, grinning, not letting up.

"No, no—I can't," he stammered out desperately, trying to manage to breathe and talk at the same time.

"Why not?"

"I can't—I can't—I can't stain these pants," he panted.

I laughed as my hand stopped moving enough to unzip his pants, releasing his cock to my waiting mouth. I slipped the whole thing down my throat, pressing my lips against the base of his shaft, my tongue licking the tip of it. It only took a minute of running him in and out before the salty cum filled my mouth.

He practically collapsed, leaning against the wall, as I wiped my mouth and stood up. Matt wrapped his arms around me, pulling me to him. "I've wanted that all day," he said, as he slid his tongue between my lips.

I pressed myself up against him, feeling the warmth of his body against mine, that particularly soft kind of relaxation you feel from someone right after orgasm, combined with the wet heat of his mouth that tasted vaguely of cigarettes and coffee. I'd wanted this all day, too.

I pushed her up against the wall, my hands pressed against the smooth fabric of her tight pants. I'd been staring at her ass in those pants all day, and all I wanted to do was shove my fingers down those pants, in her pussy, up her ass, feeling her hot wetness running down my hand, getting looser and more slippery with every thrust of my hand, priming her for the feeling of my cock rammed between her legs.

"Oh God, I've been wanting to do this all day," I panted, as my hand shoved its way past her waistband, behind her underwear, down to her crotch.

As I expected, it was already soaked, her juices coating the tops of her thighs, creating a warm puddle between her skin and her underwear. God, how I loved this girl and the way that her body responded to mine. My hand pressed against the top of her pants as I strained to shove my fingers inside, tantalized by the few inches that were allowed to me. I could feel the roughness of her closely shaved hair against my palm, in marked contrast to the delicious silky smoothness of the skin within. I could leave my hand in there forever, neatly ensconced between her lips, the tips of my fingers protected as they pushed their way inside.

I strained harder, pushing my fingers deeper into protection, until I was jolted out of my trance by the sound of a small metal clang.

"Oh shit," I said, my hand slipping out as I turned to look for the button.

"Forget it," Lanie replied, grabbing my waist with her arms and pulling me back to her, shoving her hips against my hand, pressing me back deep inside her—only now, without the resistance of the pants, I went in even farther. My fingers were in, almost to the tip of my knuckles, feeling the wet tunnel of skin curving around my cupping motions as I pressed against the wall of her G-spot, and she quivered in response.

I was so turned on that I couldn't see straight, my eyes closed to focus on the sensation of my fingers sliding in and out, as my cock pressed harder and harder against the fabric of my pants, huge and insistent, sending all sensation between my legs and to the tips of my fingers. I started to press myself against her, rubbing my cock against her hips. As if sensing what I was feeling, she grabbed my cock with her hand and started to rub. It took every ounce of control to keep moving my fingers—all I wanted was to slump against the wall and let her rub and rub and rub me to a state of total bliss. I could barely keep my fingers going as she picked up speed and pressure. I was moments away from coming.

"Oh God, I'm going to come," I moaned.

"That's fine," she replied, her fingers keeping their unrelenting pace, sending shivers up my spine and down my legs.

"No, no—I can't," I stammered out, trying to manage to breathe and talk at the same time, weakly attempting to push her hand off my cock.

"Why not?"

"I can't—I can't—I can't stain these pants," I panted. Even in this state, I had enough sense to know that I couldn't go back into the office with a white stain in such an obvious place.

The girl laughed her glorious laugh before reaching down with both hands to unzip my pants, covering my cock with the welcoming warmth of her mouth. The whole thing went down her throat. Dizzy from the pressure of her lips against the base of my shaft, from the electric thrill of her tongue as she licked the tip of it, it only took a minute until my cum shot into her mouth, the exploding tingle running through my body, as I slumped against the wall.

I wrapped my arms around her glorious body and pulled her against the wall, next to me.

"I've wanted that all day," I said, as I slid my tongue between her lips, tasting myself inside them.

She leaned against me, the pressure of her hips already starting to make me hard again. I kissed her deeper and started to think about when I could steal her away again.

A couple of days later, I got my chance. We left work separately and drove our own cars to my apartment building, meeting up with each other finally in the parking lot. I watched her get out of her car, studying the line of her pants as she turned to lock the door, the tightness of her jacket around her chest. I couldn't wait to see her with the clothes off.

I followed her as we climbed up the stairs to my apartment, my eyes tracing the curves of her ass. Her pants were as tight as her jacket, the dark denim pulled tightly across her cheeks. I let her get a few steps ahead of me, watching as the jeans wedged in her crack as she made her way up the stairs. I tried to imagine what it felt like in there, if the fabric was chafing, if the rubbing was getting her wet—was it warm in there? I could feel myself salivating like a dog as the imagery ran through my head, my nose almost at her ass, her legs sliding open at every stair.

I waited for her to notice, for her to realize that my head was inappropriately close, as my overeager libido kept demanding my fantasies be supported by a scent or a touch of something. She finally realized what was going on when we turned the second landing.

"What are you doing?" she asked, laughing.

I ran my hands over her waist, pulling her ass toward me, shoving my face against her pants.

"Aw, come on, we're almost there!"

I gave a mock growl and pressed my head in harder, taking a deep inhale of her, of the fabric, my imagination running wild with what was waiting for me on the other side of the denim.

"Come on!"

She swatted my head with her bag and scampered up the rest of the stairs. I ran after her, grabbing her as we got to my landing, shoving her against the door. She halfheartedly tried to push me off her, but I pressed harder. She looked so damn pristine, still neat from work, her hair pulled back in a tight ponytail, her milky white neck framed perfectly by the ironed collar of her blouse. I knew what was hiding underneath it all, and I couldn't wait to find it.

Tugging at her hair, I released the ponytail. Her brown mane tumbled down her shoulders as she flinched a bit from the sudden tug.

"Hey!" she cried out.

I covered her lips with mine before she could get another

word out. I wanted to fill her up with me, I wanted my tongue in her throat, my cock in her cunt. I started to pull at her shirt.

"Matt. Stop it." She pushed me away. "We're in the hallway, let's just get inside."

Sighing, I looked at her, at her wide, clear eyes. I knew what they would look like after hours of lovemaking, eyeliner smudged, hazy and erotic. I wanted those eyes. I wanted to see her look dirty. I felt my breath getting heavy as my mind triggered my mouth to salivate. Taking my eyes off her for a second, I slipped the key in the lock and let us both into my apartment.

She started chattering about our day, about our coworkers, about her meetings, but I tossed my keys to the floor, tore off my tie, and thrust her against the wall. I caught a whiff of her generic perfume as my mouth ran over her throat. My hands clawed at her shirt.

"Don't tear it," she cautioned me as she scrambled to open up the buttons.

I beat her to it, grabbing one end in my right hand and giving it a sharp tug. The buttons flew across the room.

"Hey, wha—that was my—"

"I'll buy you another," I muttered under my breath, my hands already encircling her perfect breasts, my tongue tasting her throat, her chest, her nipples. I slid my hands around her waist, moving across her ribs to her breasts. I squeezed them, gently at first, then a little harder. I could feel my energy, my desire, running into her—I could tell she was getting wetter, her nipples harder, her head tilting back against the wall. Her neck looked so perfect, so white, so virginal that I couldn't resist. I delicately ran my tongue over it, leaving little lines of saliva in its wake as I traced the line from clavicle to chin and back, and I bit.

She yelped with surprise, and I stepped back.

"That hurt!"

I smiled at my handiwork, the little red circle of teeth standing out on the freshly violated skin. I ran the fingers of my right hand over it, the left still gripping her breast. My right hand reached around her neck and pulled her close. I kissed her until I could tell that her hips were arching against mine, knowing that her underwear was getting soaked through, and I pushed her down on the bed.

She was starting to pant and didn't utter a word as I pulled her pants and underwear off, throwing them on the floor. I started to kiss her all over, my tongue and lips and teeth wet and rough, while she moaned quietly, her body stretching itself out underneath me. I slipped my hand behind her waist, down over her cheeks and between her crack. She tensed up ever so slightly as my finger firmly pressed against her asshole, lingering there before pushing inward until the tip was slightly inside of her. I let her recognize her discomfort but slid down to her pussy before she could say anything about it. I was right—she was completely soaked, the tip of my finger covered in her juices.

I removed my hand and, sitting on top of her, brought the

wet finger to my mouth. She stared at me, looking slightly embarrassed, while I slid the finger into my mouth. She tasted dirty, dirty and delicious, wet, slightly tart, and sticky. I leaned over her, my dirty finger between our faces. She blushed, while I looked at her, before plunging the finger into her mouth.

"Taste it."

I could feel her cautious tongue while I shoved my finger around, against her sharp teeth, against the soft wall of her cheeks, the slippery roof of her mouth, covering myself with slick wetness, before pulling it back out.

Quickly, I unbuttoned and unzipped. Sitting before her— naked, hard, breathing heavily—I stroked my cock in her face, just above her nose, so she could smell it. It smelled dirty and sweet as I rubbed the head against her lips. At first, she wouldn't open her mouth, but I pushed harder, and the lips parted. It was wet and warm in there, and I paused for a moment, to enjoy the feeling. I liked the feeling but not the angle.

I rolled off her, pulling her with me, so that my back was to the bed, and she was on top of me. I pushed her head down between my legs, shoving her head down and using her hair to pull her up. I could feel the tip of my cock pushing against the back of her throat. I could hear her gagging slightly, as I pushed one more time, spit seeping out of her mouth, mascara running down her cheekbones. Ah, the dirty eyes. It was good to see them again. She was panting, and so was I.

Placing her hand around my shaft, she squeezed tightly, her

spit glistening over my crotch, her lips large and red and swollen. Her neck didn't look so virginal anymore.

Matt and I left work together. He still thought it was really important to keep our affair secret, so we pulled the age-old maneuver of leaving separately, driving our own cars, then meeting up in the lot of his apartment building. I didn't mind the secrecy since I still wasn't sure where things were going between the two of us, and the fewer people who knew, the fewer people who would have to be told it was over, not to mention the fewer people who might look at me suspiciously for having sex with my boss.

Ethically, I'd be the first to admit that sex with your superior puts you in pretty dicey terrain, and, in an ideal world, nothing would ever have happened between me and Matt. But chemistry rarely follows the rules of timing or convenience, and, from the first time we were alone together, I knew there was no way I'd have the strength to walk away from this.

I remembered that every time I saw him, and this time was no different. I could feel him watching me as I got out of my car, and, without even having to look at him, my stomach clenched and my skin tingled. I'd never had a guy do this to me before, just get me totally wet without even having to touch me. Matt didn't even have to be next to me—he could be across the room, at his desk, and I'd just look at him and feel flooded with electricity. I could never get enough.

I'd obviously been turned on before, and I'd had my share of sex before, but nothing had made me feel the way Matt's desire did—it was so raw, so intense, so hungry, that it hit straight to my core, and it made my lust for him that much stronger. He'd get this look in his eyes sometimes, which was practically primal, and it made every pore on my body tighten as my stomach flipped, and my clit grew hard with need.

I loved the way he wanted me, I loved the way he could be so civilized at work, so proper with his tie, and then, alone with me, he'd become like an animal. I loved the fact that I could do that to him. It made me feel more alive than I'd ever felt before.

We were halfway up to his landing when I noticed how close his head was to my ass. I had worn my tightest pants on purpose, knowing we had plans to meet up after work.

"What are you doing?" I asked, laughing.

He ran his hands over my waist, pulling my ass toward his face, shoving his face against my pants. I knew he was probably already hard.

"Aw, come on, we're almost there!" I scolded him, trying to push his head back. I didn't want to start making out in the stairwell of his building—we spent quality time in enough awkward places at work. I wanted to get in bed.

He gave me one of his mock growls that sent shivers down my spine.

"Come on," I pleaded, as I swatted at his head with my bag and ran for his doorway.

He chased after me, grabbing my waist and shoving me against his door. I tried to push him off me, but it only made him press harder. I knew if I put up more of a fight, it would end up turning him on more, and I really just wanted to get inside and out of my clothes, so I didn't struggle too hard until he yanked at my hair. My ponytail fell out, my hair tumbling around my shoulders, and I cried out from the sudden pain.

I think my cry startled him a bit, and I used the opportunity to push him away as he was starting to paw at my shirt.

"Matt. Stop it. We're in the hallway, let's get inside." I sounded serious enough that I think he realized he'd only start getting the kind of action he wanted if he complied. Finally, he unlocked the door.

It had been a long day at work, and I was eager to have a drink before collapsing on his bed.

"Hey, Matt—what did you think of those comps the client sent over today? I thought they looked pretty good, even though they missed what we were trying to say about the younger mark—"

Before I could finish my sentence, Matt had tossed his keys to the floor, torn off his tie, and thrust me against the wall, his mouth running over my throat, his hands clawing at my shirt. The energy was primal and rough, and I loved it. I hated the fact that so much of my past had been so clean, that so many of my lovers had been well behaved. I never realized how intense it could be to feel like an animal. I knew that I had a lot to learn from Matt, that I still was restricted by way too many inhibitions and responsibility, but just being around him made me feel like I was getting dirt under my manicured fingernails, but in a really good way.

"Don't tear it," I cautioned as I unbuttoned my blouse. Primal was fine, but this was a new Donna Karan.

Before I could get it all the way off, Matt lost patience and tugged it open, buttons flying across the room.

"Hey, wha—that was my—" I cried out, trying to figure out where the buttons had landed.

"I'll buy you another," he muttered under his breath, his hands appreciatively encircling my breasts as his tongue licked my throat, my chest, my nipples. I forgot about the shirt.

He slid his hands around my waist, moving across my ribs to my breasts. He squeezed them, gently at first, then a little harder. I was starting to feel weak between the knees. Just his touch alone was enough to get me dizzy, but when he threw in a little bit of pain—that made it almost impossible for me to see straight. As he pinched my nipples, pressing them sharply between his fingers, so neatly and tightly that his fingers felt like teeth and my nipples grew red and swollen in response, I could feel the energy rushing all through me. I could feel myself wetter and weaker, and my head leaned back against the wall as my knees buckled and my clit ached.

He ran his tongue over my throat, and I moaned, thinking I might drown in the sensation.

And then he bit me—sharp daggerlike teeth, out of nowhere, piercing my skin with their sharp blades. I yelped with surprise, and he stepped back.

"That hurt!"

He smiled, not an ounce of apology anywhere on his face. In fact, he looked quite pleased with himself. I wanted to kick him. It really had hurt, and I knew how easily I bruised. I'd have to wear scarves and turtlenecks for days to avoid the inevitable nuisance of office gossip.

Matt delicately ran the fingers of his right hand over the injured area, clearly inspecting his handiwork. His left hand was still on my breast, as his right hand reached around my neck and pulled me to him for a kiss that quickly became all I could think about.

He kissed me again and again, always deeply but alternating between rough and soft, his tongue shoving its way down my throat, as though searching for something or lightly prodding the roof of my mouth and the backs of my teeth. The pain disappeared as I pressed myself against him, my hips craving his, my body trying to find as much contact as it could. I started to wish he'd rip my pants off the same way he did with my shirt. I rubbed myself against him, desperate to make him attack me again, and he pushed me onto the bed.

As my hips felt his, and my pelvis felt the pressure between his pants, my hands wrapped around his waist, my nails scratching along his back. On cue, he reached between us and unbuttoned my pants. Throwing them aside, he started to kiss me all over, his tongue and lips and teeth covering my skin with the trails of his saliva, the little bites sending electric fire throughout my skin.

He slipped his hand behind my waist, down over my ass, and between my crack. I tensed up despite my efforts not to—I knew how much my ass turned him on, but I still couldn't get into it. Every time his fingers drifted over there, I grew ever-so-slightly terrified that he'd decide now was the time to experiment and shove them inside. He lingered there while I could feel myself waiting nervously, his finger just outside, and then he pressed the tip inward. I cringed at the strangeness of the sensation, the odd discomfort of feeling something going in when it should be going out. I couldn't tell if I liked it or not, it just felt bizarre and unexpected. Luckily, his fingers kept moving, slipping down into my pussy, and my body expanded with relief and pleasure, arching myself onto his fingers and pressing them farther into me.

Playing coy or just difficult, just as I pressed his fingers into me, Matt slipped them out and straight into his mouth. He stared straight at me as he licked them. I realized that I'd never tasted myself before, and I must have looked startled as I wondered what he thought. He leaned over to me, his finger between our faces, and I could feel the red blush spreading across my face. Sometimes Matt could make me feel like such a prude. It wasn't that I was a prude, though—it was just that I'd never done this kind of thing before.

"Taste it," he ordered, cutting into my thoughts.

He shoved his finger into my mouth, against my teeth, against my cheeks, the roof of my mouth, moving so quickly I could barely figure out what I tasted like—sort of sweet and bitter and milky at the same time—and then the finger was out again, as Matt impatiently tugged his pants off.

Sitting in front of me, he started stroking his cock in my face, just above my nose. I could smell the fact that he hadn't showered since yesterday—it smelled earthy and dirty as he rubbed the head against my lips. He was so hard and the look in his eyes was so intense, that, after a couple of seconds, it didn't matter what he smelled like, and I let him gratefully slip inside my mouth.

He paused for a moment as I ran my tongue over the head and the shaft, feeling how hard he was and letting my knowledge of his desire start a leaking between my legs.

He rolled off me, pulling me down with him, so that his back was to the bed and I was on top. He forcefully pushed my head between his legs, shoving my head down and using my hair to pull me up. I winced. I hated this part. I hated, hated, hated it. I really loved going down on him, every fantasy I had always included a scene with his cock in my mouth, but I hated the way he pulled my hair and shoved me. I hated being told what to do and how to do it. I hated it when he got rough like this, when I felt manhandled and degraded and like an animal.

I could feel the tip of his cock pushing against the back of my throat, and I gagged slightly. He let up a bit, pushing again but more gently, his hips arching off the bed as his swollen cock tried to squeeze itself into my mouth. I could feel his desire running in a straight line from his cock to my throat to my legs. The more he shoved against my face, the more his need for me sent heat through my body. His need was turning him into an animal, and I started to feel like one in return.

There was something so primal about him as his brain focused on nothing else besides what was happening in my mouth, as his eyes glazed over, lost in a world between my lips. Every inch of his body lay at the mercy of my mouth. There was no thought involved. Everything degenerated to its simplest level—pain, pleasure, need, desire.

I was feeding him. I controlled him.

As he shoved into me, there was nothing between us other than the urging of his cock. I felt his body pressing into mine, his dick against my throat, his balls against my hand. Nothing else mattered. I had ceased to become anything for him other than a vehicle of desire. That revelation released me. We were animals together. I felt like a porn star, and I started to love it.

His cock pressed into my throat, my tongue against the shaft, my lips tight over my teeth, my pressure meeting his, I forgot about everything else. I forgot about work and my shirt and the marks on my neck and whether I'd remembered to call my mother back, I forgot about it all and just thought about the pressure of his cock in my mouth and my lips against my teeth and the way his hand gripped my hair. Nothing else mattered but his desire for me and my desire for him and the rough, tumbling pain of it all.

I placed my hand around his shaft, squeezing tightly as I began to rub, my spit glistening everywhere, my lips large and red and swollen. I was a porn star.

She started to rub, slowly at first and then picking up speed, her breasts swaying back and forth as she hovered over me. I watched hypnotized for a couple minutes, feeling the building sensation between my legs, until I had enough—I was about to come, and I was definitely not ready for this to be over.

I grabbed her around the ribs and pulled her up, pushing her over to my side, her back on the bed, as I looked down on her.

"What do you want to do?"

I just stared at her, briefly placing my forefinger over her mouth, cautioning her not to open until I said so. I grabbed my tie, which I had discarded earlier, and quickly looped it around her wrists and the bed's headboard. She started to say something, but I gave her another silencing look.

I ran my finger down her forehead, over her chin, past her neck, her chest, her stomach, slowly looking her over. Her arms stretched out above her head, the taut biceps slightly clenched, the wrists looking especially small and frail against the dark gray of my tie. She had her head tilted up, a bit defiant, daring me to make my next move, and it only made my hunger stronger. I ran my finger over her arms, across her chest, over her hips, savoring the sensation, dragging out the moments in tight anticipation.

Her brown hair strewn across the pillow, her body lean and long and completely exposed, the white skin looking ivory against my sheets, perfect lines accentuated by the jarring tuft of her black pubic hair. She was there, and she was all mine.

With a quiet groan of pleasure, I pushed myself into her. She flinched slightly at the suddenness of it, but that only made me feel more alive. I started pounding right away, in and out, fast and hard, the wincing on her face accelerating my need. Her mascara running, her eyes closed, her hands clenched around the fabric of my tie, I kept thrusting, watching as her breasts danced back and forth, echoing my rhythm.

She felt tight and wet and soft and hot, and I couldn't slow down.

"What do you want?" I growled at her between thrusts.

She opened her eyes and looked at me, startled, her body vibrating as I pounded into her.

I asked her again, louder.

"I want—I want," between her uncertainty and the panting, it was almost impossible for her to get anything out.

"Do you want me to fuck you?" I asked loudly, my face inches from hers, my hips continuing to shove impatiently against her.

"I want—I want," she was still struggling to get the words out.

I asked her again, louder, every other word accentuated with a push in, every other corresponding word with a pull out.

"Yes, yes, yes, I want you to fuck me!" she shouted back at me, her eyes gleaming and defiant. "Now!"

It was over in a matter of moments. My pace accelerated near the end until, with one last deep heave, I could feel myself about to come. I pulled out right before, letting my cum shoot all over her smooth skin, splattering the white fluid across her stomach and chest and breasts. She was mine, and I had marked her.

Her mouth opened as I finished, and I sent the last bit of spray into it. She licked her lips with a grin and wriggled her arms.

"How about letting me out?"

I untied her and lay down. She was still wet and leaking onto the bed. I couldn't resist slipping my fingers back into where I had just been, shoving in and out and watching her moan. It didn't take long before her hips were pressing against my fingers, and she was pleading with me not to stop. I didn't stop, I kept my pace, riveted by the look of exquisitely straining pleasure and concentration on her face. She came with a shudder and a moan, the muscles pulsing inside her, her hips shivering as her body collapsed.

She wrapped herself against me, a plethora of wet and hot thank-you's whispered in my ear. I wasn't listening, I was already thinking about what I wanted to do with her next.

I started to rub, slowly at first, then picking up speed. I could feel his cock hardening in response, my fingers sliding over the spit I'd left behind. I grew hypnotized by my movements, lost in my own rhythm, until Matt suddenly grabbed me around the ribs and pulled me up, pushing me over to my side, my back on the bed.

"What do you want to do?" I asked, not certain what he expected from me.

He just stared at me, briefly placing his finger over my mouth, as though telling me to keep it shut. He grabbed his tie off the floor and quickly looped it around my wrists and the bed's headboard. I started to ask what he had in mind, but he gave me another one of his looks, and I decided to wait and see what happened next.

He ran his finger down my forehead, over my chin, past my neck, my chest, my stomach, slowly looking me over. I felt chills as his eyes made their way across my body. I stared back at him, daring him to make his next move. He still said nothing, just running his finger over my arms, my chest, my hips, as I felt myself getting hotter and sweatier, but I was determined to make him make the first move.

I wasn't going to ask for anything. I knew he desired me, and I'd let him take me on his own terms. I wanted to find out what they were.

I didn't have long to wait. With a quiet groan of pleasure, he pushed himself into me. I flinched slightly at the sudden shock of having him pressed inside and flinched again as he started pounding into me, but the harder he shoved, the wetter I got. Within seconds, he was smoothly sliding in and out. My eyes closed, I gave my body over to what was happening between my legs.

"What do you want?" he growled at me between thrusts.

I opened my eyes, startled.

"What do you want?" he asked again, louder.

"I want—I want—" He was pounding so hard, I couldn't get the words out.

"Do you want me to fuck you?" he asked loudly, his face inches from mine, his hips unrelenting against me.

"I want—I want—" I couldn't get the words out. I needed him to stop, just for a second, so I could catch my breath.

He only asked me again, even louder.

I rose to the challenge. I sucked in enough air to fill my lungs, and shouted back at him, "Yes, yes, yes, I want you to fuck me! Now!"

He came pretty quickly after that. His pace accelerated near the end until I felt like he was a machine, and I was a corresponding unit—a dizzying sequence of in and out. He gave me one last deep heave and pulled out, just in time to shoot his cum all over my skin, splattering his white fluid across my stomach and chest and breasts like a dog claiming his territory. I was his, and he'd marked me.

My mouth opened as he finished, trying to get one proper breath of air, but he quickly seized the moment to send the last bit of his spray into it. I licked my lips and grinned—predictable bastard.

"How about letting me out?" I asked, wriggling my arms as a

reminder. I was hoping he wasn't going to think it was some clever game to leave me tied up for a couple of hours.

Luckily, that idea hadn't occurred to him, and he untied me before lying down. I wondered if he was going to notice that I was still wet and leaking onto the bed, or if I'd have to point that out to him. I didn't—he clearly couldn't resist slipping his fingers back into where his cock had just been, shoving in and out, watching me moan. I was so wet and so swollen that I didn't mind his roughness. I craved his roughness. My body pressed against his hand, trying to get him in deeper. I begged him not to stop, the slow wave of pleasure already starting to gather in my toes. He didn't stop, he kept his pace, and I came with a shudder and a slow moan, my muscles quivering against his hand, my hips shivering as my body collapsed against the bed.

I wrapped myself against him, lost in the delicious sensation of postorgasmic warmth and the soothing softness of skin on skin. "Thank you," I whispered in his ear, my arms around his chest, my legs draped over his. I felt safe and loved and desired. I felt satisfied.

Even though I got to stare at him the whole next day, we didn't have a minute alone. We had presentations and client conferences straight through from morning on, so there was no opportunity for any personal conversation. Matt was too busy running the show to give me more than the occasional perfunctory glance or the professional acknowledgment, but I got to stare at him the entire time. One of the added benefits of falling for people that you work with is that it makes all-day meetings that much more entertaining.

While Matt droned on about schedules and comps and interface strategies, I idly stroked my pen across my page and stared at him. He had these great intense brown eyes and dark, almost black hair that he kept well slicked and well kept. His mouth was almost too big for his face, and if he hadn't been so animated, his teeth might have appeared too large and dominating—but his face was so lively, his head sort of perpetually cocked to one side or another, his teeth constantly flickering in a charming grin, that it all seemed to fit, accentuated neatly by his aggressive jawline.

I kept looking at that jawline, and the mouth that it carried, and I kept thinking about how that mouth felt on mine, and what the inside of that mouth tasted like, and how the tongue felt, against my teeth, against my breasts, between my legs. I couldn't follow anything that came out of that mouth, the entire meeting was lost on me, as I kept crossing and uncrossing my legs, hoping no one could tell that my nipples were hard against my bra, knowing that no one could tell my underwear was stained, but wondering if people could see the flush on my cheeks and desperately praying that no one would ask me any questions about anything because all I knew was that the muscles of Matt's upper arms couldn't have been any more defined against the fabric of his shirt.

I kept sitting there, pen to paper, watching the movements under his shirt, knowing what that body looked like, and breathlessly waiting for the time when I could see it again. Every once in a while, just when I would least expect it, Matt would look over at me and hold the glance just three extra seconds, and shivers would run down my spine, my pussy would leak all over my panties, and my stomach would flip. I'd have to cross my legs again and hope no one wondered why my cheeks were so pink.

At a couple points, I contemplated excusing myself to go to the bathroom, wondering if maybe, if I took care of myself on my own, I'd feel calmer for the rest of the meeting and not quite so hungry for every one of his glances. But I scrapped that idea every time it came up, knowing full well that any personal satisfaction would feel woefully inadequate compared to my fantasies, compared to the reality of what I knew an encounter with Matt was like.

So I sat there and waited it out, useless to the meeting, but watching Matt's every move, wondering when he'd say something, do something, anything to indicate that he knew what I was feeling and that maybe he felt the same way.

If he did, he didn't let on. He just kept carrying on with the meeting and his presentations—his white button-down shirt neatly rolled up at the wrists, just casual enough to seem unpretentious but still pressed enough to look like he meant business—directing his flirtatious charm at the client, occasionally directing a question or a comment to one of the members of "our team," but performing like charisma oozed out of his pores. And I, like every one of our clients, sat there, eating it up, and wanting more.

Before I realized it, it was 6:00 P.M., and Matt's hand was on my shoulder.

"Is that all right then?"

I stared at him blankly.

"Perfect," he said, his hand rubbing my shoulder in a charmingly affable manner before walking away to shake the client's hand and escorting them out of the office. "I'll be right back, don't go anywhere," he called over his shoulder, giving me one quick wink on his way out.

I had no idea what he was talking about, so I just sat and waited for his return, pen drawing loose circles on my otherwise blank notepad, my mind continuing to concoct fantasies of what Matt and I could have done in the conference room all day—if we'd just been left alone.

And then the door clicked shut. I looked up and smiled. Matt was grinning back at me.

"I knew you wouldn't mind."

"Mind what?"

"You know, staying late tonight to make the quick revisions to the comps so that the client can present them at the big meeting tomorrow."

Apparently, I had completely missed that part of the conversation, but anything that involved staying late with Matt sounded good to me.

"So that's okay then?" he asked, a naughty look on his face.

"Sure. Of course. That's fine."

He sat on the table next to me, his finger tracing my cheekbone. "I figured we could order some dinner, make the changes, and then have a little time to ourselves . . . ?"

"Sounds good to me," I said, my mind too caught up in what that could mean to worry about whether I sounded like an idiot or if my cheeks were turning an eager pink again. I ran my hand down his thigh, resting lightly on his knee before making my way slowly back up. "What do you want to eat?"

Lanie and I had one of our all-day client meetings the day after we'd fucked at my apartment. It was, in fact, during one of those endless meetings that I first decided I wanted to fuck her. I could feel her watching me while I walked the client through some Power Point presentation, could feel her staring at me longingly while I spewed out P&L figures and discussed CRM strategies. She made me feel powerful, and I could tell that whatever it was that she was feeding me made the client love me all the more. By the end of that meeting, I had the two of them in the palm of my hand—Lanie watching my every move, her eyes adoring, the client ready to sign whatever I put on the table. It was brilliant.

I became the master of the surreptitious study, keeping my eyes on Lanie while addressing the client, grinning inwardly at what Lanie did when she thought I couldn't see—at the careful hiking of her stockings, the casual adjustment of her hair, the awkward fidgets with her blouse, the dreamy twirling of the pen. I particularly enjoyed startling her when she was in the midst of one of her more intense reveries—when I knew her mind had probably concocted some elaborate situation which involved me fucking her ass against a white leather couch—then I'd turn to her and ask her if she agreed with my assessment, if she had anything to add, or if she thought we should break for lunch.

Every time, without fail, she would do the same thing: her eyes would blink up at me, like a startled deer, a pink blush would steal across her cheeks, she would bite her lower lip in consternation, before nervously pushing her hair behind her right ear—or if she was wearing a ponytail, she'd just stroke the flyaway strands back to their place—then emit some affirmative, fumbling response that gave every indication she had no idea what question I'd asked.

I loved it. It was like a game. The predictability of it all just made it more perfect—it became a challenge to make it happen, and a quiet score when the events occurred in their intended, appropriate order.

This went on for a couple of meetings, stretching out over a period of a couple of months, before I made any sort of move. When Lanie first joined the company, I was fucking this Brazilian blonde who worked for Human Resources and loved wearing a leash when we were alone together. She got really into degradation, and after a while it got boring. There's only so much you can do with someone who so clearly just wants to be abused or dominated, and so I had to end it after finishing my list. She didn't take it very well—she'd gotten pretty accustomed to being told what to do—so I had to get her transferred to Seattle, which left time open for Lanie.

As soon as she'd come to interview, I knew I wanted her. There was something about her pristine preppiness, about her awkward but well-groomed confidence, her perfect hair and her immaculate design portfolio that made me want to get her dirty. I wanted to make her scream and moan. I wanted that makeup smeared across her face. I wanted her blouse ripped. I wanted to see those perfect stallion legs spread out beneath me, bucking for more. I wanted her hair tangled across my pillow. I wanted to shove myself into that neat, tight opening and feel her raw wetness against me. I wanted to feel her manicured nails across my back. I wanted to make her beg for me, and I wanted to make her want whatever I decided to give her.

I took my time. I was carefully charming—nice, but not too nice. I watched myself intrigue her. I played it cool, but I sucked her in. I'd smile at her as I walked by her desk and watch her drop her pencil. I'd take the elevator down with her and listen to her try to make conversation while I looked calm and detached, giving her one of my easy grins as I walked out to my car before wishing her good night. I noticed as she gradually stopped paying attention to the content of our meetings and started paying more attention to me. I made sure to compliment her work at least once a week and rest my hand on her shoulder at least once a meeting. I combined my fatherly praise with a devilish charm, and she didn't stand a chance.

The first time I asked her if she wanted to grab a drink, I knew she'd had other plans because I watched her hurriedly cancel them. I made her feel like a princess, buying her drinks and pretending to be riveted by tales of her childhood, her apartment, her family, her grad school days. I let my eyes crinkle up in boyish amusement at her pathetic stories, I kept her martini glass full, and I let my hand rest on her arm or her thigh at every opportunity. I had her in the palm of my hand.

I played it perfectly, though—dropping her off at her house with a quick kiss on the cheek and a chaste "see you at work" good-bye. She had no idea what to think. I knew she'd spend the whole weekend conferring with all her girlfriends about what to do, deconstructing my every move in an attempt to reach some kind of understanding. I didn't call because I knew that was what she wanted.

I waited until Monday morning, then I didn't speak with her. I made sure to get to work early, so that I was already there when she walked in. I'd strewn all my papers over my desk and didn't even look up as she went to her desk. I could tell by the way she gripped her handbag that she felt very ill at ease.

Perfect, I thought.

I didn't talk to her until lunch, when I walked by her desk on the way to the copy machine. I gave her a curt good morning, leaving before she could say more of the same. Her eyes followed me, and I could feel her desire adding inches to my height, energy to my already confident demeanor. I waited until Tuesday to stop by her desk, giving some innocuous compliment as my excuse. Her face lit up when I praised the interface, and she couldn't have grabbed her notebook any faster when I invited her to join the client meeting that afternoon.

She stared at me that whole meeting and, when I took her home that night, let me fuck her in my kitchen, on the bed, and against the couch.

I invited her into every meeting after that, knowing that her adoring gaze made my charm even more effusive for the client, knowing that having her watch me like that made me feel like king of the world, and knowing that no one, when I was like that, could resist giving me what I wanted. This meeting was no different. She twirled her pen across the page, her eyes trained on my every move, completely useless in terms of professional contribution, but priceless when it came to my ego.

I sailed through the presentation, half my mind on the figures and the assets, the other half already imagining what I'd do to her that night. I played all my moves, more to keep myself busy than to reel her in—I already had her exactly where I wanted her. It kept me occupied, while droning about marketing strategy, to startle Lanie periodically, watching the predictable blush and ensuing hair adjustment, watching the inevitable crossing and uncrossing of the legs every time I rested my hand on her shoulder, letting the mood heighten to keep the energy electric, and my confident charm where it needed to be to get me through the four hours of Power Point.

By the time six o'clock rolled around, my preoccupied mind had already figured out what it wanted to do with her.

I told the client it wouldn't be any problem to make the necessary revisions to the comps before tomorrow's meeting, knowing that it would take less than hour to make the required changes and knowing that it would be an easy excuse for keeping Lanie in the conference room after everyone else went home.

"Is that all right then?"

She stared at me blankly. The poor dear had been too captivated by my Hugh Grant grin to hear a word I'd said.

"Perfect," I continued, ignoring the fact that she hadn't replied, my hand rubbing her shoulder in a charmingly affable manner before walking away to shake the client's hand and escort them out of the office.

"I'll be right back, don't go anywhere," I called over my shoulder, giving her a quick wink on my way out.

I knew she had no idea what I was talking about, and I knew she'd be sitting there, waiting for my return, wondering what it was she'd just agreed to, her mind coming up with several promising scenarios, her underwear probably getting damp just at the prospect. I took my time, shaking hands and making idle conversation near the elevator bank, letting her sit alone in the conference room with her fantasies.

She smiled at me eagerly as I walked back in, closing the door shut behind me.

"I knew you wouldn't mind."

"Mind what?" she asked nervously.

"You know, staying late tonight to make the quick revisions to the comps so that the client can present them at the big meeting tomorrow."

I let my words hang there while she wondered if I had ulterior motives or a strictly professional attitude. I gave her about fifteen seconds to try to figure it out.

"So that's okay, then?" I asked, letting a naughty look slide across my face.

"Sure. Of course. That's fine." She could barely get the words out between the big grin.

I sat on the table next to her, my finger tracing her cheekbone. "I figured we could order some dinner, make the changes, and then have a little time to ourselves . . . ?"

"Sounds good to me," she said, her cheeks turning an eager pink. She ran her hand down my thigh, resting lightly on my knee before making its way slowly back up. "What do you want to eat?"

Sucker. It was almost too easy. I wondered if I'd have to get her transferred to Seattle, too.

I made her work on the comps just long enough to convince herself that she'd read me all wrong. When we first started, she thought I was kidding, but I let on no sign of any humor at all—I was all business, cool and professional—until she resigned herself to the same sort of attitude. Once I'd scored that quiet victory, I suggested Japanese.

"Sushi sounds great," she exclaimed, relieved by the distraction.

I placed the order from my desk and came back to the conference room, having confirmed that we were the only ones left in the office. I sat on the edge of the table and loosened my tie.

"I thought that meeting went well."

"Oh yes, definitely!" She glowed at me.

"Did you like my suggestion about teen market strategy?" I asked, my left foot starting to stroke her right calf.

"Absolutely. Totally on track." She pushed her hair behind her left ear.

I hadn't said anything about teen market strategy during the meeting.

"Oh good."

I took my tie off and starting wrapping it around my left wrist in an apparent display of distraction, but I knew exactly what I was doing. I wrapped it around my wrist, then carefully unwrapped it, wrapping and unwrapping as I watched her watch me.

I steered the conversation to innocuous matters, talking a bit more about today's meeting, about Sally's design idea, about the client's proposal for additional work that spring, about Bill's attitude toward the company—mindless topics I generated while

I kept wrapping the tie and while my left foot kept moving against her calf. I wanted to create just enough tension that she wouldn't be able to keep her mind on her sushi.

The food arrived fifteen minutes later, and I carelessly tossed my tie on the table between us while I paid the bill. I let Lanie unpack it as I organized the paperwork, bringing back to my desk everything I'd need for the next morning.

We ate a couple pieces each before I started dipping the rolls in the sauce and feeding them to her. She took my lead, and soon we were each feeding each other, laughing as we struggled to keep the rolls intact between our chopsticks, to keep the soy sauce from dripping on each other, to keep the ginger from falling on the table—and then, of course, the tragic mistake! One particular piece, en route to her mouth, lost a couple drops of soy sauce on her white thigh. She quickly moved to wipe it with her finger, but I stopped her with my hand. While she finished chewing what was already in her mouth, I put my chopsticks back on the plate and pushed her chair away from the table.

Getting down on my knees, I carefully, slowly, licked up the errant soy sauce. I licked up the sauce and kept licking my way up her thigh, my tongue tracing the salty residue across the width of her leg, pushing my head up her skirt until I reached her underwear. It was already damp. I shoved my tongue against it, feeling her thighs tense up and a slight moan release from her mouth.

"What do you want?" I asked, my head still between her legs.

"What's that?" she asked, jolted out of her daze.

"What do you want?" I asked louder, pulling my head back and resting my hands on either side of her chair, my fingers gripping the armrest. "What do you want?" I asked even louder, my face inches from hers.

She cowered back slightly.

"Do . . . you . . . want . . . me . . . to . . . fuck . . . you?" I asked, drawing out the words, the saliva starting to gather in my mouth in anticipation. "DO YOU WANT ME TO FUCK YOU?" I shouted.

She nodded quickly, too nervous to do or say anything else. My hands on the armrests, I stood up fully, towering over her as she seemed to grow even smaller. "I'm waiting for an answer," I said calmly.

"Ye-yes," she stammered.

"Yes, what?"

"Yes, I want you to fuck me," she whispered.

"I can't hear you."

"Yes, I want you to fuck me," she said, louder, doing her best to look me in the eye.

"Good," I said, smiling. I looked at her for a second before letting the smile slip off my face. "Now get up," I ordered, pushing the chair away from me with a sudden shove, the wheels sending her flying into the wall behind her.

As she hit the wall, her head jerked back, and she jumped off the seat. She'd never seen me like this, and I could tell she didn't like it, but I also knew her well enough to know she'd never try to leave. She stood against her chair, looking at me nervously.

"Come here, honey," I said sweetly, motioning with my finger for her to come closer. "Come here and give me a kiss." I gave her another of my easy, charming grins.

She gingerly stepped toward me. When she got within reach, I grabbed her around the waist and pulled her close. I gave her one long, penetrating kiss, my tongue pressing into her mouth, my arms clenching her so tightly she could barely breathe, before spinning her around and pushing her down on the table. I pushed her hard enough so that she hit the table with a solid whack, but not so hard that she'd actually be hurt or have a bruise.

Holding her head down on the table with my left hand, I reached over with my right and pulled her skirt up and her underwear down. Her ass was gorgeous, all exposed and white, underwear around her ankles, her thighs looking firm, and her butt looking perky and round and delicious. I could feel myself getting rock hard against my pants. She wasn't making a sound.

I ran my finger over her ass, down her thigh, and between her legs. Despite the nervous look in her eyes, she'd leaked all across her pussy and across the tops of her thighs. I leaned over and took a big lick, my tongue going up her thigh, across her pussy, and between her cheeks. She was clean—all I could taste was the pungent tanginess of her juices and the slight mustiness of her body.

71

She gave another slight moan as I ran my tongue over her again, licking up the fluids that were seeping out of her, feeling the hot softness of her lips, her swollen clit, the warm hole of her insides. She tried to push up from the table, but I held her down more firmly with my left hand as I ran my tongue around the outside of her asshole. I could feel her tense up, but I didn't care.

While I licked, I unzipped my pants with my right hand and started to rub myself. I was already hard, but I rubbed back and forth, quickly and lightly, until I couldn't possibly have gotten any harder, until I knew I was as solid as I could get, then I took my hand and shoved it between her legs. I pushed it into her, first one finger, then two, then three, feeling her tightness slowly expand as I pressed more insistently. I shoved myself in and out several times, letting her get looser and wetter, coating my hands with her slippery liquid. When she felt lubed and hot, I pulled my hand out and shoved my cock in.

Oh, she felt good. Her head still pressed on the table, her ass at a perfect ninety-degree angle, just the right height for me to ram myself in and out. It couldn't have been any better. The sight of her perfect white panties, crumpled around her ankles, fallen around her neat black heels, just made me hotter, just made me want to shove even harder into the perfect preppy ass.

"Do you want me to fuck you?" I growled into her ear.

"Yes, yes," she stammered.

"SAY IT LOUDER."

72

"YES, YES," she shouted back.

I pounded into her, feeling her hips hitting the table underneath me. My hands were around her waist, my thumbs pressing into her ass, leaving little red fingermarks behind them.

"What do you say, bitch? Do you like it?"

"Yes, yes!"

"Do you like getting fucked this way?"

"Yes, yes!"

"Do you like getting fucked like a dog?"

"Yes, yes!"

I was starting to get bored, so I pulled out and flipped her over. I wrapped my left hand around her hair and held her head to the table, while my right hand ripped her shirt open. I bared my teeth and went for her—my cock shoved between her legs, and my mouth went for her neck. I thrust into her, harder and harder, while I sucked the life out of her neck and her breasts and her shoulders and arms. I knew she'd be covered in little bruises by the next morning, and I didn't give a fuck. I knew she'd figure out some way to hide them, and all I was concerned with was getting as much of her as I could inside my mouth.

I hadn't thought Matt was serious about getting the comps revised that night, but I guess he was, because we worked on them for almost an hour, the odd thigh-to-thigh contact or a prolonged moment of eye contact the only clues that more might happen later. Other than that, I tried to ignore my increasingly impatient stomach and libido, hoping that the sooner we finished our work, the sooner I'd be able to satisfy one or the other.

I definitely appreciated what Matt was doing for me—outside of the bedroom as well as in. I knew it wasn't my professional experience that got me into these client meetings—I knew Matt kept me there to keep his ego boosted and to fulfill his Girl Friday fantasies—but whatever the reason was, it still got me there, and, until my sexual desire got the best of me, you better believe I made the most of it. I turned myself into a sponge during those meetings, I absorbed every little thing I could. Matt may have been a good fuck, but he was also a brilliant designer and an amazing negotiator. Sitting in those meetings was an intensive course in everything I wanted and needed to learn, and I did my best to pay attention at all the relevant points and to stare adoringly at all the others—except, of course, until all I could do was stare adoringly at him.

Before my brain went between my (and his) legs, I sat there and watched and listened, and I saw him handle clients like putty, turning on the right grin and the right tone until they thought they were calling the shots, when really they were asking for everything he wanted. I saw him get his way every time, I saw him convince them to do it all his way, and he made it look effortless. The simplest designs were always the most shocking, the most striking, and I made mental notes of every technique in his book.

After a month of all this, I could see my work improve, and I started to create a whole new portfolio, a "post-Matt" portfolio, full of designs I never would have pulled off without this kind of guidance and inspiration. I learned about colors and lines and accents—all basic technique I'd learned in grad school, but Matt had an approach that made everything look cleaner, more defined, more stylized. I sat in those all-day meetings and thought about style, his and mine, and where it could all go. I watched him run the show, studying every move, remembering it all for future meetings, for future presentations when I'd be in the front of the room, when it would be my designs the clients couldn't wait to approve.

I thought about all that, and I thought about how fucking him was a small price to pay for a priceless education—an especially small price to pay for the fact that I was starting to really enjoy our sex life. I hadn't so much in the beginning, then it was more about the turn-on of fucking your boss, of hearing Mr. Sophisticated panting in your ear, of seeing him arch his back while you licked his cock, but now I was starting to get into it.

I'd never done anything like this before—all my previous sexual partners were solid and reliable and certainly didn't try to grab my ass in the elevator. It had never occurred to me that I wanted anyone to grab my ass in an elevator, but now that Matt had started, I realized that I kind of did. Part of me liked his primal qualities, the marked contrast between his slick work demeanor and the absolute dog he carried around inside.

What was interesting about the whole thing was that, while I learned about the finer aesthetics of design, I also learned that

I had a bit of dog inside me. All my other lovers had been modest and conventional and, frankly, I'd never thought a hell of a lot about sex. I enjoyed it, when it was done right, and I put up with it, when it was done wrong—but I'd never had a partner that made me forget who I was. My constant self-awareness would temporarily disappear with Matt and, while I would have preferred it sometimes if he didn't get off on making me feel nervous or afraid, there was something about being taken outside of myself, about being so consumed in the animal passion of the moment, to which I was starting to get addicted.

So I sat there in meetings, alternating between intellectual reflection on the startling new way Matt had approached interface design or information architecture and feeling myself blush as I remembered how he'd thrown me over the couch the night before and fucked me like a dog, and I'd feel myself blush both at how much I'd enjoyed it and how much I wanted it again.

So I worked on the comps with him, trying to keep my mind on all things corporate, while time got later, and I got hungrier. After we finally made enough headway for Matt's satisfaction, he suggested we order Japanese, and I enthusiastically agreed. He went and placed the order while I prepared the materials for delivery the next morning.

"I thought that meeting went well," he said, sitting on the edge of the table and loosening his tie.

"Oh yes, definitely!" I exclaimed.

"Did you like my suggestion about teen market strategy?" he asked, his left foot starting to stroke my right calf.

I had no fucking idea what he was talking about. "Absolutely. Totally on track." Even if he knew I was lying, I figured he wouldn't care enough to call me on it.

"Oh, good."

He took his tie off and starting wrapping it around his left wrist, wrapping and unwrapping while his eyes stared into mine. God, sometimes I thought he knew me better than I knew myself—he could play me like one of his damn toys. All it took was the sight of that tie slipping around his arm, and I could barely see straight. I clenched my thighs together in an attempt to lock in the waves of heat that were rushing out of me.

Luckily, Matt steered the conversation to irrelevant office politics and innocuous matters like the client's proposal for additional work that spring, and I allowed myself the luxury of smiling and nodding while I contemplated the imminent arrival of food and the satisfaction that was sure to come, both during the meal and after.

When the food arrived, I dug into it, eating several satisfying pieces before Matt and I started dipping the rolls in the sauce and feeding them to each other. We laughed as we struggled to keep the rolls intact between our chopsticks, to keep the soy sauce from dripping on each other, to keep the ginger from falling on the table. And then, of course, the inevitable—one particular piece, en route to my mouth, lost a couple drops of soy sauce on my thigh. Before I could wipe it with my finger, Matt stopped me with his hand. While I finished chewing what was already in my mouth, he put his chopsticks back on the plate and pushed my chair away from the table.

Getting down on his knees, he carefully, slowly, licked up the errant soy sauce. He licked the sauce and then kept licking—up my thigh, tracing the salty residue across the width of my leg, pushing his head up my skirt until he reached my underwear. I knew it was damp, and I knew he could tell. He shoved his tongue against it, and my thighs tensed up from the effort of try-ing to keep from tearing off my clothes and throwing myself on top of him.

"What do you want?" he asked, his head still between my legs.

"What's that?" It was taking every ounce of self-control not to shout, "Shove something inside me, dammit."

"What do you want?" he asked louder, pulling his head back and resting his hands on either side of my chair, his fingers grip-ping the armrest. "What do you want?" he asked even louder, his face inches from mine.

I cowered back slightly. I didn't like it when he got so loud.

"Do . . . you . . . want . . . me . . . to . . . fuck . . . you?" he asked, drawing out the words, the saliva starting to gather around the edges of his mouth in anticipation in a way that al-ways reminded me of a rabid dog. "DO YOU WANT ME TO FUCK YOU?" he shouted.

I nodded quickly, too nervous to do or say anything else. Even though I didn't think he'd ever hurt me, I still couldn't get used to this part of his act. His hands on the armrests, he stood up fully, towering over me as I could feel myself growing smaller.

"I'm waiting for an answer," he said calmly.

"Ye-yes," I stammered.

"Yes, what?"

"Yes, I want you to fuck me," I whispered.

"I can't hear you."

"Yes, I want you to fuck me," I said, louder, doing my best to look him in the eye.

"Good," he said, smiling. He looked at me for a second before letting the smile slip off his face. "Now get up," he ordered, pushing my chair away from him with a sudden shove, the wheels sending me flying into the wall behind me.

As I hit the wall, my head jerked back, and I flew off the seat. What the fuck was he doing? He'd never done anything like this before. I couldn't tell how he wanted me to react. I didn't know if I'd just make it worse for myself by trying to leave—if any sign of struggle would just get him more fired up—or if by staying calm I'd infuriate him further. I looked at him nervously, trying to gauge what my next move should be.

"Come here, honey," he said sweetly, motioning with his finger for me to come closer. "Come here and give me a kiss." He gave another one of those damn grins.

Even though he terrified me when he got like this, those grins still made my heart stop. I closed my eyes and took a deep breath. Why was I doing this to myself? Why didn't I just leave him? Why was I such a fucking sucker for what was little more than a spread of sparkly white teeth? I wanted to punch myself. I didn't need this shit. I didn't need him—I didn't need him to teach me about design, I didn't need him to teach me about fucking. I was doing just fine before I met him.

What the hell are you talking about, Lanie? You weren't doing fine. You were miserably bored. Your design work sucked. You were a step away from designing corporate intranets. You got your good-night kisses from David Letterman and *Friends* reruns. You went to the same bars and fielded the same pickup lines from the same guys wearing the same ties. You needed Matt to fuck you against a wall. You needed someone to throw you against the wall. You needed someone to remind you of what it was like to live life when you weren't always comfortable, when you weren't always bored.

I stepped toward him cautiously. When I got within two feet, he reached out and grabbed me around the waist, pulling me close. He gave me one of his incredible, long, penetrating kisses, the kind where I couldn't breathe because his tongue was so far down my throat and his arms so tightly around my chest, before spinning me around and pushing me down on the table. He pushed me so hard that my head hit the table with a solid whack and, for a second, all I could register was the pain that shot through my head, down my neck, and across my shoulders. I could feel it in my fucking toes.

Holding my head down on the table with his left hand, he reached over with his right and pulled my skirt up and my underwear down. I was starting to feel irritable. My head throbbed. I wanted to push him off me, but I was afraid that would just make him hold me down even harder. I started to think about what would happen if I left him—I'd probably have to get another job. One of my friends had warned me about letting my boss fuck me, but I'd decided to do the one reckless thing I'd ever done, and here I was. So what if I had to get another job? At least I had one hell of a portfolio to show for my time here.

The mental overview of my résumé was interrupted by the sudden sensation of his finger running over my ass, down my thigh, and between my legs. Fucking chemistry. It didn't matter how much he pissed me off, something about the way he touched me, about the feel of his finger against my flesh made my skin catch on fire, made me feel hot and wet and desperate for more.

He leaned over, running his tongue up my thigh, across my pussy, and over my ass. Oh God. The pain in my head had vanished, replaced by a pulsing pressure between my legs. I barely heard the moans coming out of my mouth as he ran his tongue over me again, licking up the fluids that were seeping out of me, over my swollen clit and inside me. I couldn't stand it. He was giving me just enough pressure to make every part of me want to scream but not enough to bring me anywhere close to satisfaction.

I tried to push up from the table—I wanted him to fuck me and get it over with—but he just held me down more firmly with his left hand as he ran his tongue around the outside of my asshole. I started to tense up. This part always made me nervous. I knew it was the prude in me, but I always had a terrible feeling that the perfect climax for Matt would have to involve sodomy, would probably involve fucking me from the rear like a dog, and it made me cringe every time I thought of it.

Luckily, that wasn't Matt's fantasy of the moment as, without any warning, he suddenly shoved his hand between my legs, first one finger, then two, then three. I was so wet by that point, the three fingers slipped right in. He pushed them in and out several times as I got looser and wetter and hotter, my hips bucking toward his hand, until he finally pulled his hand out and shoved his cock in.

Oh God, it felt amazing. Despite the bullshit and the ego, the inexcusable violence and the occasional immaturity, Matt knew how to fuck. He fucked me like no art school student ever had. He fucked me like no honor roll candidate had. He fucked me like I'd always imagined a man could fuck, I just never imagined them fucking anyone like me. He fucked me until I felt raw, he fucked me like he couldn't help himself and like I couldn't either. There were no apologies. There were no reservations. He fucked me like we were animals—despite the fact that I was still wearing my Kenneth Cole heels and was pressed up against a shiny, lacquered conference room table.

"Do you want me to fuck you?" he growled into my ear.

"Yes, yes," I stammered.

"SAY IT LOUDER."

"YES, YES," I shouted back.

He pounded into me as my hips hit the table. His hands were around my waist, his thumbs pressing sharply into my ass. The combination of pleasure and pain was leaving me blind.

"What do you say, bitch? Do you like it?"

"Yes, yes!"

Suddenly, with no warning, he pulled out and flipped me over. Wrapping his left hand around my hair and holding my head to the table, he ripped my shirt open with his right hand. I didn't give a fuck. He bared his teeth and went for me—his cock between my legs, his mouth on my neck. I felt like meat, like a delicious piece of meat that was being savored and consumed and devoured. I'd never felt like this before, certainly not before Matt. Sex had always been so neat then. I knew I was going to get bruises all over my neck and breasts and shoulders and arms, but I didn't care. I'd fucking wear a scarf. I'd call in sick. I'd call in sick and tell Matt to come over and fuck me back to wellness.

"Come here," he said, grabbing me forcefully and pulling me off the table.

I shook my head, trying to gather my thoughts, bending over to pull my underwear back up.

"We're not going anywhere. Leave them down there."

His fingers wrapped around my wrist, Matt dragged me behind him to the end of the conference room while I tried to keep up as best I could, taking the little awkward steps allowed to me by the confines of the underwear around my ankles. He pulled me across the room until we got to the far end, then he shoved me in front of him, against the wall.

I stood there and looked at him. I had no idea what he had in mind. My underwear was at my ankles, my skirt still intact at my waist, my shirt at the other end of the room along with my bra. My hair hung around my face, a big rumpled mess that bore no resemblance to the ponytail it had been earlier. I stared at him and waited for him to make his move.

He just stood there and stared back at me.

We looked at each other, my eyes on his, his eyes traversing my body, evaluating me as though I were up for purchase. I was determined not to make the first move, plus I was interested in seeing what exactly he had in mind. He kept looking until his eyes suddenly lit up. I watched him with curiosity as he darted back to the table and started fooling around with the projector.

Suddenly, a very white, very intense light shone directly into my eyes blinded me. I raised my hand to cover them, squinting to try to see what Matt was doing, but he shouted at me to put my hand down.

"I can't see anything!"

"I don't care. You don't need to see anything."

"Well, what am I supposed to do? Just stand here?"

"Yeah. Just stand there. Just stand there and let me look at you."

What a freak. Okay. That was easy enough. I stood there, my eyes closed, waiting for him to get bored with this game.

"Touch yourself," he commanded.

"What?"

You heard me. Touch yourself. I want to watch."

"Just like this? Right here? Right now?"

"Yes. Now. Think about me fucking you and let me watch."

Well, this was certainly a first. I'd never masturbated in front of anyone before, and certainly not in the center of a spotlight, half-naked in my company's conference room, at the request of my boss—but what else was I going to do? I wasn't going to say no.

I leaned back against the wall, eyes closed, and slipped my right hand between my legs. Oh God, I was so wet, aching from the past several hours, that I knew it wouldn't take me long at all. I alternated between pushing my fingers inside me—feeling them fill me up, curving my hips against them until I could hit my G-spot with my forefinger—and running them in tight circles against my clitoris. In and out, in and out, round and round—it didn't take long until I'd forgotten about Matt and the projector and the client meeting that had taken place where I was standing. It didn't take long until I was completely absorbed in my motions, lost in the rhythm of my fingers and the sensation of steadily increasing heat.

I took my other hand and grabbed my left breast with it, fingers tight around the nipple, pulling and pinching until it got as hard as my clit felt, tingling and hardening from my touch. I could feel the pressure building inside me, and my efforts intensified. I pushed harder, shoving my fingers deep inside me, my mind completely focused on the release that I could tell was moments away.

My legs started to tremble, and I slumped farther against the wall as my entire body started building to orgasm. I knew I was shaking, and I could barely keep my balance. I clenched my teeth to keep from screaming as the sensation started around my toes. The blood was pounding in my ears as I threw my head back against the wall, uttering a long, deep moan as my legs almost gave out underneath me.

I could hear myself panting hard as the contractions starting to subside. My eyes opened, groggy and heavy-lidded, but the white light just made me close them again. My body slumped against the wall, my fingers still inside me, feeling the muscles slowly relax, twinges of electricity running down my thighs at every touch. I smiled to myself, lost in the bliss of the moment. Matt was silent.

"Come here," I said, grabbing her forcefully and pulling her off the table. I wanted to look at that damn bitch properly.

She shook her head as she bent over to pull her underwear back up. Yeah, fuck that, I thought.

"We're not going anywhere. Leave them down there," I told her.

My fingers wrapped around her wrist, I dragged her behind me to the end of the conference room. I pulled her to the far end and shoved her in front of me, against the wall. She looked like a street whore. There was no sign of her upbringing, her class, her education. There was nothing proper about her now. The only sign of what she might otherwise look like was the fact that her shoes were impeccably polished. Other than that, with her mascara-smeared eyes staring at me beneath a tangle of hair, no one would ever know who she was or where she'd come from. My dick got hard just thinking about it.

I stood there and looked at her. It was perfect, but what did I want to do next? Her skirt was still primly around her waist, but I loved that part. I loved the fact that she was half-dressed. It made it more exciting, more interesting—this poor little Orphan Annie waiting to be abused. I stared at her while I tried to figure out what I wanted.

Then I had it—I knew exactly what would turn me on even more, what I'd love to see and what I'd love to make her do. I ran back over to the conference table and unplugged the projector from the laptop, shifting it so that it pointed straight at her, then turned it on. She raised a hand to cover her eyes, but I told her to put it down.

"I can't see anything!" she whined.

"I don't care. You don't need to see anything."

"Well, what am I supposed to do? Just stand here?"

"Yeah. Just stand there. Just stand there and let me look at you.

"Touch yourself."

"What?"

"You heard me. Touch yourself. I want to watch."

"Just like this? Right here? Right now?"

She was totally freaking out. She had probably never masturbated in her life, and, even if she had, I'd bet money she'd never done it in front of any of her uptight pussy boyfriends.

"Yes. Now. Think about me fucking you and let me watch."

She leaned back against the wall, eyes closed, and slipped her right hand between her legs. I watched her face and her body and her hand, and it made me hard just to see the look on her face as those fingers went in. She was so wet, they just slipped through, and, as she kept moving, her head leaned farther back, her body slumped against the wall, completely lost in the sensation. I could tell it didn't take long for her to forget I was there.

I watched her alternate with her fingers—pushing them in and rubbing her clit—while I thought about how her insides must feel, how hard her clit must be, and how incredible the sensation of pushing my dick in there. When she took her other hand and grabbed her tit with it, fingers pulling and pinching her nipples, I thought I was going to lose it, I thought I was going to come right there in the room. I grabbed my cock in my hand and started to rub myself. I didn't care if I came before she did or after or whatever the fuck. I couldn't stop. It was so hot just to look at her, to imagine what she felt like, the heat of her insides, the heat that must have been coming off her skin—I leaned against the conference table and ran my hand up and down my cock—harder and faster, my movements matching hers.

Her legs started to tremble, and she slumped farther against the wall, her entire body starting to build to orgasm. I watched her shake, and I could feel my thighs shaking, too. My cock was so hard—it felt completely solid. I watched her come, quivering so hard that she could barely keep her balance, and I couldn't help it—I stopped rubbing myself and just watched. She clenched her teeth to keep from screaming—one habit I still hadn't managed to break—as she threw her head back against the wall, letting out a long deep moan as her legs almost gave out underneath her.

I watched her pant, ignoring the nagging hardness of my cock. That could wait. Her eyes opened briefly, all heavy-lidded, but quickly closed again. Her body slumped against the wall, her fingers still inside her, as she slowly started to relax. She smiled to herself while I thought about how striking her body looked in that light, how perfect against the dark wall, and I pictured what my cum would look like, sprayed all over like a Pollock painting.

* * *

I walked over to her, still leaning against the wall, and told her to get down. She knelt on all fours and looked up at me obediently.

"Suck it."

Perfectly trained, she didn't hesitate, taking my huge cock in her mouth and running her tongue back and forth. The pressure built up as her lips closed around it. I could feel the tips of her teeth running along the edges, and it drove me fucking wild. My hips started bucking against her mouth, and I pushed her head right up against me. With one hand holding her hand and the other pressed against the wall for balance, I shoved myself in and out of her, faster and faster and faster, until I could feel myself about to come, and then I quickly pulled out, sending my spray shooting out over the wall behind her.

She turned around to look at the arc of dripping white that the projector illuminated on the gray wall.

"Taste it."

She took her finger and gingerly dipped it in one of the larger drops of cum before slipping it into her mouth.

I watched her face, concentrating, as she licked the rest of it off her lips.

"Now clean it off."

She looked at me, uncertain.

"Go on. You heard me. There's a client meeting tomorrow. Get that shit off there."

She gave me another uncertain look before turning around to get to work. She started off just cautiously running her finger along the end of the arc but then, after a sly look at me, leaned close to the wall and started licking. She ran her tongue from start to finish, slowly, languorously, her eyes going back and forth between the wall and mine. I could feel my cock getting hard just watching her. I could tell she was getting into it. She pressed her face against the wall, her ass sticking out at me, her red tongue and her red, red lips leaving wet trails behind them on the wall, licking up every trace.

He walked over to me and told me to get down. Curious as to where he was going with this, I knelt on all fours and looked up at him, awaiting further instruction.

"Suck it."

Ah yes, I knew what to do with that one. I took his cock in my mouth and ran my tongue back and forth, building up the pressure as my lips closed around it. I ran the tips of my teeth along the edges, just grazing his skin—not so as to leave a mark but so as to give him just enough sensation to make his thighs clench up and to make him grab my hair with his hands as he moaned. His hips started bucking against my mouth as he shoved his cock farther into my mouth. With one hand holding my hand and the other pressing against the wall, he shoved himself inside and out of me, faster and faster and faster until his cock felt like it was going to burst and my lips felt swollen, and the precum and saliva were dripping out of my mouth.

Then he quickly pulled out, spraying his cum all over the wall behind me.

I turned to look at the arc of dripping white that the projector illuminated on the gray wall behind me.

"Taste it."

I took my finger and gingerly dipped it in one of the larger drops of his cum before slipping it into my mouth.

He watched me as I slowly, in true exhibitionist fashion, licked the rest of it off my lips, before looking at him for further instruction.

"Now clean it off."

I wasn't exactly sure what he meant with that.

"Go on. You heard me. There's a client meeting tomorrow. Get that shit off there."

This was definitely something we'd never done before, but one of the reasons I was with this damn guy was to do precisely those kinds of things, so what the fuck? I turned around and started licking—cautious, at first, because I didn't know how dirty the wall was, but then, after confirming that this cum didn't taste any different than cum that had gone straight into my mouth, other than perhaps a slight dusty aftertaste, I sort of started to get into it. The performer streak in me loved being watched doing just about anything, and this was easy enough.

I ran my tongue from start to finish, slowly, seductively, watching him watch me, my eyes going back and forth between the wall and him. I knew his cock was getting hard just standing there. I pressed my face against the wall, my naked ass in perfect spotlit view, my tongue leaving wet trails behind it. I knew I'd never have another boring meeting in this conference room again.

She was ahead of me in the hallway, her hand about to reach for the door, the keys dangling in her right hand, when I first saw her. I quietly darted down the hall, leaning over to whisper in her ear.

"Can I join you?"

I loved locking us in the company bathroom, pulling off just enough of her well-pressed work clothes to stick my dick between her legs and to suck her nipples into red little points, before sending her back to her desk, my fluids drying on her skin. I thought of it as a little prep run before our evening sessions, a way to warm myself up and to get her even more distracted.

"Sure, why not," she replied, letting us both into the room.

We went in, and she locked the door behind us. I grabbed her from behind, rubbing myself against her tight ass, my hands gripping her breasts, panting against her neck. God, I loved feeling my dick against her perfectly pin-striped pants. She turned around, and my cock slid between her legs, my tongue between her lips, my hands racing all over her body. I wanted to fuck her senseless.

And then I thought of something I'd rather do.

"Don't move," I told her, as I reached my left hand into my pocket.

"What are you doing?" she asked, a hint of fear and a lot of suspicion in her voice. My right hand was still inside her, and I could feel her tensing up around it.

"Just relax." I tried to keep my voice soothing, my tone even, as I slowly slid my left hand out of the pocket, trying to keep the noise and rustling to a minimum.

"What have you got there?" She craned her head, trying to see what I had hidden in my fistlike grip.

"You'll see. You'll see. Just don't move."

"Show me," she said, her tone growing more authoritative. My left hand had almost reached my right when she slammed her thighs together, imprisoning both hands between them. I was impressed by how tough her grip was—all those hours of aerobics had paid off.

"Show me," she repeated, the muscles of her thighs clenched so tightly, I could clearly see their definition. It made me hard just looking at it. I realized that I liked it when she stood up to me.

Just to see what she'd do, I gave a sudden tug with my left hand to pull it out of her viselike grip, but, just as quickly, she swooped her right hand down and wrapped her fingers around my wrist.

"Show me, you motherfucker. What have you got in there?"

Her fingers were so tight around my wrist, I could already see the skin turning pink. Crazy little bitch. I loved it.

"Let me go, and I'll show you."

She studied me for a second, the gears turning in her head, before she released my wrist.

"Okay. There you go. Now show me."

I slowly unfolded my fingers to display two small binder clips in the palm of my left hand. They were the metal kind, with a red center and little metal wings that swooped down to hold stacks of paper together that were too big for ordinary paper clips.

"And what the fuck are you planning on doing with that?" she asked, her tone still more authoritative than scared.

I grinned at her. "Why don't you let me show you?"

"You've got to be fucking kidding me. Anything you'd do with those clips will never be pleasant. What sick, twisted idea of a good time have you come up with now?"

"Why don't you let me try?" I used my best wheedling tone, keeping my eyes sparkly and my grin charming.

"Try what, exactly?"

"Let me try, and if it hurts, we'll stop."

"You'll stop?"

"I'll stop."

"Promise?"

"Promise."

She sighed for a second.

"Do you really get off on this?"

"Yes, yes, I do," I replied, giving her another of my Hugh Grant grins.

She sighed again, like an indulgent mother, and it made me want to hurt her all the more.

"Come on. Let me try. If it hurts too much, I'll take them off."

"Okay. Fine. Do it. Let's get it over with."

This time, the grin was genuine. Reaching between her legs, I used two fingers from my left hand to spread her pussy lips open, using the rest to carefully snap a clip on each side. As the metal clamps closed on, she shuddered, her fingers gripping my shoulders, her nails digging into my skin. I stayed there, motionless, waiting to see what she would do. The fingers tightened for a moment and then, slowly, began to relax. Cautiously, I looked up to see what expression might be on her face. There was a look of intense concentration, her eyes shut, her cheeks tight—she looked almost preorgasmic. I stood up. She didn't move. Her eyes stayed closed.

I let the two of us hang like that for a minute, her fingers gripping her thigh, watching the look of concentration, waiting to see what her next move would be. She slowly opened her eyes and looked at me.

"I kind of like it."

I didn't know what to say to that—that certainly wasn't what I expected.

"You do?"

"Yeah," she said, drawing out the word as if she couldn't bear to let it go. "Yeah, I do."

"Do you want me to take them off?"

"No, no, I don't," she replied thoughtfully. "I'd like to keep them in."

"You do?" This was bizarre.

"Yes, I do." She stood up carefully, gingerly pushing her skirt back down to her knees, leaving her underwear at her ankles.

I reached forward to pull them up for her.

"No, don't." She stepped forward and out of them, leaving them on the floor behind her. "I'm not going to put them back on."

"You're not?"

"No. You can keep them for later. I'm going to go back to work. I want to keep the clips on—at least for now." Leaning over, she gave me a quick kiss on the cheek. "I'll see you after work," she said, closing the door behind her, leaving me alone in the bathroom, my pants still around my ankles.

The key was in the lock, my hand on the doorknob, when I felt his breath on my ear.

"Can I join you?" he asked.

I smiled to myself. Our company had a single-stall bathroom, and Matt and I had used that privacy for fucking during business hours before. This was nothing new, and nothing that I'd ever turn down. I loved the distraction, both during the act, then sitting back at my desk, feeling the drying wetness between my legs, traces of him still on my thighs.

"Sure, why not," I told him, letting us both into the room.

We went in, and I locked the door behind us. He grabbed me from behind and started rubbing himself against my ass, his hands gripping my breasts, panting against my neck. I closed my eyes and just felt his hot heat, letting his tense energy fill my body, before turning around to press my tongue into his mouth. His hands were all over me and mine all over him.

Then he suddenly pulled back. I looked at him strangely. What's going on?

"Don't move," he told me, as he reached his left hand into his pocket.

"What are you doing?" I asked, knowing that I couldn't hide the nervousness in my voice. Matt wasn't like the boys I'd dated in college—I could never manage to play it cool around him. His right hand was still inside me, and it made me feel nervous to know that it was in there while his left hand was up to something I couldn't figure out.

"Just relax."

Yeah, in whose dreams? Every time Matt tried something different, it made me increasingly skeptical about his motives and even more suspicious about mine. Why was I doing this to myself? Why was I dating a guy who was clearly such a sadist? What was so wrong with me that he managed to turn me on as much as he did?

"What have you got there?" I craned my head, trying to see what he had hidden in his fist.

"You'll see. You'll see. Just don't move."

"Show me," I said, the fear and frustration started to mix with simple annoyance. If he was up to something, the least he could do was respect me enough to tell me what he had going on. His left hand was snaking between my legs when I slammed them together, clamping down on both of his hands. At the very least, this fucker wouldn't think I was easy.

"Show me," I repeated, the muscles of my thighs clenched tightly around his wrists.

The little bastard gave a sudden tug with his left hand, slipping it out from between the grip of my thighs, but using good varsity lacrosse coordination, I swooped my right hand down, wrapping my fingers around his wrist.

"Show me, you motherfucker. What have you got in there?" My fingers were so tight around his wrist, he had to feel the pain. Tell me what you've got in there, I thought. Tell me.

"Let me go, and I'll show you."

I looked at him for a second, wondering how sincere he was—or was this just another game? I took the chance and released him.

"Okay. There you go. Now show me."

He slowly unfolded his fingers to display two small binder clips in the palm of his left hand—the same kind I had in the top drawer of my desk, the same kind I used to fasten my proposals together.

"And what the fuck are you planning on doing with that?" I asked, more annoyed than scared. This wasn't even kinky fun—this was just kinky wrong.

He grinned at me. "Why don't you let me show you?"

"You've got to be fucking kidding me. Anything you'd do with those clips will never be pleasant. What sick, twisted idea of a good time have you come up with now?" Who the hell did this guy think he was?

"Why don't you let me try?" He kept grinning at me, as if this was the most delicious secret party we'd ever had. I wasn't falling for it. I didn't know what he had in mind, but those were fucking binder clips. They didn't belong anywhere on my body.

"Try what, exactly?"

"Let me try and if it hurts, we'll stop."

"You'll stop?" I had to admit, I was skeptical.

"I'll stop."

"Promise?"

"Promise."

I sighed for a second, wondering what twisted childhood had surfaced with these bizarre fetish obsessions.

"Do you really get off on this?"

"Yes, yes, I do," he replied, unable to get that damn grin off his face.

I sighed again. I knew if I didn't at least let him try, I'd never hear the end of it.

"Come on. Let me try. If it hurts too much, I'll take them off."

"Okay. Fine. Do it. Let's get it over with." How much could it possibly hurt? And if it really hurt, well, then, I'd make him take them off. And if he wouldn't take them off, I'd take them off myself—it wasn't like I was tied up or anything.

Reaching between my legs, he used two fingers from his left hand to spread my pussy lips open, using the rest carefully to snap a clip on each side. As the metal clamps closed, I shuddered, the wave of pain racing from my pussy through my heart and chest to my fingertips and toes. I gripped his shoulders tightly, breathing in sharply, waiting for the shock and the sensation to subside. Get a grip, I told myself. It's just pain. I kept breathing, my eyes closed, the pain so acute it felt tangible—like red waves knocking against me and rolling up my skin.

And then, slowly, the waves began to subside. The pain fell into the background. It refocused. It left my fingers and toes and chest and retreated back between my legs. My pussy felt alive, somehow. It felt larger and fuller and acknowledged. I felt like I had discovered some part of me that had always hidden behind the rest of me, behind my upbringing and my clothes and my fears. I felt like Matt had just swung open Door Number Three, and my pussy was there, ready to meet me. We had finally been introduced, and I felt all the more powerful for it.

I slowly opened my eyes and looked at the man who had brought me here.

"I kind of like it."

I could tell this wasn't at all what he'd expected—either from the situation or, especially, from me.

"You do?"

"Yeah," I said, barely able to talk, so lost in this newfound sensation and this newfound realization. "Yeah, I do."

I didn't need Matt anymore to show me what I'd been unable to find on my own—I'd just found it, and I knew I'd never lose it again.

"Do you want me to take them off?"

"No, no, I don't," I replied thoughtfully, the words coming out of my mouth almost as much of a surprise as my enjoyment of the sensation. "I'd like to keep them in."

"You would?"

"Yes, I would." I stood up carefully, gingerly pushing my skirt back down to my knees, leaving my underwear at my ankles. It was time to get back to my desk.

He reached forward to pull my panties back up.

"No, don't." I stepped forward and out of them, leaving them on the floor behind me. "I'm not going to put them back on." I wanted to sit at my desk, the air going directly under my skirt. I wanted to feel the air on my pussy, the air and the pain and the metal all blending together in one intoxicating mess.

"You're not?"

"No. You can keep them for later. I'm going to go back to work. I want to keep the clips on—at least for now." Leaning over, I gave him a quick kiss on the cheek. "I'll see you after work," I said as I closed the door behind me, leaving him alone in the bathroom, his pants still around his ankles. I'd still see him after work, but everything would be different now.

I sat at my desk and felt the metal pressing into my skin. It made me feel Amazonian somehow, more alive. Sex had always just been something you did to end dates, an escalated kiss, a goodnight routine. I'd never thought of it as a form of communication before. I'd never thought of it as a way to express myself. Now, though, the curtain had been pulled back, and I couldn't believe everything that had been hiding behind it.

I liked sex. I really liked it.

What else? Oh yeah, I figured out that the actual literal act of sex, of the cock pushing its arrogant way into my vagina, was only a very, very small part of the whole show. There was so much more involved. It was all the other stuff that you could really sink your teeth into. It was all the other stuff that made me wet, that made me leak onto my chair while my clips made sharp reminders against my flesh, and my underwear waited for me somewhere in one of Matt's pockets.

I could see Matt at his desk out of the corner of my eye—he was talking on the phone with some client, an image of pure professionalism. I smiled to myself, wondering where, exactly, he'd stashed my urine-stained panties, and if one of his hands had slipped into his pockets to hold them as he chattered about upcoming deadlines and delivery schedules. I smiled to myself at his little reminder of our escapade while I shifted my thighs to remind me of mine.

I knew I'd take the clips out on my own. I knew that I wanted that bathroom trip to be a private one, where I would slowly remove them and then gently massage my sore and swollen lips, feeling the delicious sensation you can only get from overstimulated skin. I'd massage my lips, then, leaning against the bathroom door, my fingers would drift from the outside of my pussy to the inside, slipping their way into me before slipping back out to rub circles around my clitoris. It would be a different orgasm than the kind I got with Matt—it would be slow and gentle and sweet and full of the perfect kind of self-awareness you only get when you make love to yourself.

And then, then I'd go back to work, waiting to see what the evening would provide.

When Lanie left me in the bathroom with her dirty underwear, I didn't quite know what to do with myself. It wasn't at all the way I'd expected the episode to turn out. I don't know exactly what I'd expected, but it wasn't this. At the very least, there would have been some coming on my part, something to properly conclude our interaction—not being left behind in the bathroom alone with my cock and her underwear.

I stared at her panties, at the faint urine stains drying while I looked, and I stared at my cock, which grew harder the longer I debated what to do next. Even though I didn't know what it was that I wanted, something about the stains turned me on, and I damn well knew I wasn't satisfied with the way things had turned out.

I looked at her crumpled underwear, at the pale yellow droplets on the white satin, and I figured—fuck it. I just started to jerk off. While my right hand was doing its job, my left hand picked up the underwear and hung it neatly on the doorknob. I picked up speed, watching them swing gently on the metal handle. As a little game to keep myself amused, when I was just about to finish, I shifted my body and aimed just perfectly enough so that my cum sprayed neatly into the underwear, collecting in a little pool above some of Lanie's stains. I watched the white liquid gather and grinned to myself. Fuck that bitch and her perfect little panties that weren't so perfect anymore. No, now they bore witness to the events of the day and the little travails I had arranged for them.

I washed my hands while the cum dried, then, wrapping the panties neatly in a paper towel, I stuck them in my pocket and returned to my desk. I had phone calls to make.

"Check out the interface designs when you have a moment."

The stack of paper fell on my desk with a thud, landing between Trina's coffee and my keyboard.

"I'm sorry?" I asked, looking up at Lanie.

"When you have a moment, I'd like your opinion on the interface design."

I nodded, unable to stop staring at the red binder clip that was holding it all together. "Trina and I are just talking about the new online promo project, but I'll look it over as soon as we're done."

"Sounds great," she replied, flashing me a neutrally professional grin before turning away. "Oh, they start on page five," she called out over her shoulder, with just the hint of a smirk on her face.

What was she up to? While Trina resumed her corporate chatter, I surreptitiously thumbed my way through the stack of paper—page five, page five, where are you? I found page five just by the farthest edge of the page, still trying to give Trina the impression that I was listening to every word she was saying. I could see the tip of a little Post-it note in the middle of a page. Dammit. I wanted to know what it said, but I couldn't figure out a way to look without Trina peering curiously over my shoulder.

I'd have to wait.

Wrapping it up as quickly as I could, I approved half of Trina's ideas, suggested modifications to a third, and rejected the rest. I nodded through her platitudes and agreed to have lunch next week to discuss matters further. I could have been a robot for all the good I was doing—yes, yes, no, no, we'll see, try that one again, sounds good, really, yes, yes, okay, excellent, perhaps try that one again . . .

Finally, she was gone, and I opened right up to page five.

"Drinks. Your place. Eight."

My cock hardened just reading it. I traced the edge of the red clip with my fingers. Was it one of hers? I brought the papers to my nose and sniffed—it seemed like there was a hint of her juices, but that could have just been my overactive imagination. I leaned back in my chair and thought for a minute. What was going to happen tonight? The sassy little princess had never had quite so much sass. Part of me was irritated since I didn't like changes I didn't control, but part of me wondered if maybe, just maybe, the real fun with Lanie was to start. I did enjoy a good fight, and it had always been a point of disappointment that I broke my girls down so quickly.

Regardless, I wrote myself a note to ask Trina if she wanted to move next week's meeting from lunch to dinner.

"Drinks. Your place. Eight."

I scribbled the words on a Post-it note and slapped it down in the middle of a stack of paper. Times had changed. I was calling the shots. I marched over to Matt's desk, interrupting his little flirt session with one of the new designers, dropping my interface sketches halfway between her coffee and his keyboard.

"Check out the interface designs when you have a moment."

"I'm sorry?" he asked. Matt was never very good at handling

unexpected developments or interruptions. He liked to be the chief choreographer of his own little charades. When other people started moving in on the act, he either forced them out, enrolled them in his training program, or bowed out for more satisfying endeavors. I was curious to see how he'd handle my new agenda.

"When you have a moment, I'd like your opinion on the interface design," I repeated.

He nodded, unable to take his eyes off the red binder clip that was holding it all together. It wasn't one of mine—I was saving those for myself—but I'd chosen one of the same size and color just to get his little brain (and dick) going.

"Trina and I are just talking about the new online promo project, but I'll look it over as soon as we're done."

Ha. I would have bet money that the new online promo project was the last thing from either of their respective minds, but I just smiled cheerfully at the two of them.

"Sounds great," I said, turning away. "Oh, they start on page five," I called out over my shoulder—let that ruin the rest of Trina's time with him. I knew he wouldn't be able to hear a word she said until he'd figured out what I was up to.

I could hardly wait.

I rang the doorbell, the nerves in my stomach mixing with the adrenaline in my veins. I was ready for this, I'd been waiting my whole life for this, but there was still the nervousness of something new that put an edge onto my thrill. I didn't know who I was anymore, but I was more than determined to find out.

I tapped the heel of my stiletto while I waited for him to open the door. I'd had these shoes in the back of my closet, left over from some college Halloween party years ago, and this seemed like the perfect night to reintroduce them. I wore them around the house sometimes, for my own amusement, but other than that one drunken party, they'd never really served the purpose for which they were intended—yet.

When the door swung open, I kept my eyes fixed on his, watching them scroll up and down my body, registering my glee at the shock he was unable to conceal. I knew how I normally dressed, and I knew how he stereotyped me for it. The strappy black stilettos with the razor-sharp heel, the sleek black vinyl coat zipped up to my neck, my hair pulled back in a ballerina bun—it definitely wasn't the Lanie he'd expected.

"Aren't you going to ask me in?" I asked, pushing my way past him. The time for pleasantries was over. The time for niceties and folded legs belonged to scrapbooks and fond memories. I'd found something new.

"Uh, yeah, um, sure . . ." his voice trailed off as he stood in the foyer, staring as I unzipped my coat just enough to let him suspect there wasn't much to speak of underneath, but not quite enough for him to confirm that fact.

"Close the door. Come make me a drink."

He shook his head, as if to loosen the daze from his eyes, and shut the door. Trying to regain his alpha male status, his voice slid back to masculine ease while he opened his liquor cabinet. "What can I fix you?"

"Vodka. On the rocks."

The drinks took him a minute to prepare, then he turned to me expectantly. I grabbed mine from his right hand and swallowed it with one shot. He blinked at me, his glass awkwardly untouched in his left hand.

I grinned at him. I'd never seen this side of him, and he sure as hell had never seen this side of me. I hoped the vodka would keep me going for a while longer. I figured the more I pretended I knew what I was doing, the more he'd think I did, and the more I could pull off this charade. Sometimes becoming who you are is as simple as acting like what you want to be.

"I think it's time to get started."

He just blinked at me again.

"Finish your drink," I told him, pointing to his left hand. He looked down at it like he'd never even noticed he had one. With a couple swallows, the drink was gone, the glass on the cabinet, and his eyes back to blinking at me.

All right, Lanie, you can pull this off. Just keep coasting on your adrenaline, and you'll be fine, everything will fall into place if you just get started.

Without shifting my gaze, my right hand slid under my chin, grabbing hold of the big metal zipper resting against my chest. With a big tug, the zipper raced down to my knees, and the coat swung open. Matt just stared. The coat fell to the floor. It took every ounce of self-control to keep my mouth from splitting into a grin. I had to maintain appearances.

I stood there for a moment, letting his eyes take in my naked body, the white skin broken only by my black garter belt and thigh-highs. Other than that, and the black leather wristbands, also left over from the Halloween costume, I was stark naked—but I'd never felt more confident.

Leaning over to him, I put my mouth right next to his ear, just like he'd done to me so many times before. "I want you to fuck me," I whispered.

"I want you to fuck me," I said again, louder. I slid my hand around his back and pulled him close to me with a sudden motion. "Fuck me now."

Then I slipped my hand back around as quickly as it had gone there in the first place, slipped it right round to his stomach, and pushed him soundly against the wall. With my hand pressed against his stomach, my heels bringing my eyes to the level of his, I brought my lips right next to his and flicked my tongue over them before repeating, "Fuck me. I want you to fuck me."

My hand was still against his stomach, still pressing him against the wall, my face up close to his, our lips almost touching but not quite—we were so close but the distance could still have been measured by nonmathematicians. We were in separate spheres, and I towered neatly in mine on my perfect heels— "Why don't I wear these more often?" I thought.

He still hadn't said a word.

I slowly moved my hand down his stomach, over his pelvis, and cupped it around his crotch. His dick was hard, and it pressed against my hand in response. Perfect. Everything was going according to plan.

"Come on, Matt," I purred. "Don't you have anything to say? Don't you want to . . . fuck me?"

"Yes, yes, of course, I do." As the words came out, some of his macho confidence seemed to return—the head tilted back up, the eyes more judgmental, the shoulders higher.

"Then let's get to it," I exclaimed, a mixture of joy and impatience—my hand grabbed his belt buckle, and I pulled him into the bedroom.

Less than a minute later, he was totally naked, but I was still wearing my heels and garter belt—I was keeping those on for moral support, inspiration, and to help further the illusion of control.

Control. It was all about control, or at least the illusion of having it. That's what I kept reminding myself.

I got on the bed and pulled him on top of me. His cock was hard between my legs, eagerness all over his face, the confusion at this change of pace still evident but desire overriding everything.

"Come on, I can't stand it," I cried to him, wrapping my heeled feet around his waist, locking them behind his back, as I pulled him into me.

It didn't take long for him to find his rhythm, for him to find a steady pace, for him to get lost in the motion of it all as he forgot the bizarre circumstance that got him there in the first place. I kept my legs wrapped around him, my thighs and calves elements of the larger machine the two of us had created. Sure, of course, I was being fucked like I'd been fucked before—but I was fucking back like I'd never fucked back before.

It's not that I'd been a total cold fish up until now, but I'd always been a bit reserved. I'd always held a part of myself back, using the same self-moderating technique I learned when I was eight, and my mother told me never to cry in front of strangers. There was the public you and the private you, and the private you stayed behind locked doors. It stayed private, which meant no one saw it. You were civilized and respectful, you kept your clothes clean and your dry cleaning in plastic bags, you ate your salad with the right fork, you never pushed or shoved, you never asked for more than your share, and you always said thank you when you got it.

But now? Now everything had changed. It wasn't that I had forgotten the rules, it wasn't even that I had eradicated them so completely that I didn't feel a tiny bit aware of my irresponsible behavior. I still felt the twinges of middle-class guilt, but I knew what I was doing, I knew I was asking for more than my share, that my clothes were getting dirty, and I was finally feeling alive.

Somehow, I'd lived my life without learning that sex should never be tidy unless it was supposed to be boring—and if it's boring, shouldn't you just turn on the television instead? Sex is not meant to be neat. Sex is not designed to be proper. If your sex is tidy and neat and proper, well, then you're not doing it properly. Sex is about fucking, it's about getting dirty. And if your clothes are taken off the right way, if they land on the floor and under the bed, if they're taken off so that you're naked, you're stripped down, well then, go with it. Lose yourself along with the pretenses of your pleated pants.

Fucking isn't pretty. It's what animals do. It's what we do to be animals. I'd finally figured it out, and it felt glorious.

My thighs, my calves, my feet, my hands—everything pulled him to me, pressed him in deeper, building our way to some hypnotic high of shoving and pulling and pressing and thrusting, and we were animals. We were skin and flesh and nails and hair and thrusting harder and harder, and I held him close, digging into his flesh, pressing against him, willing him in harder and faster, and we were moving together in perfect tandem, our bodies wet with sweat, our panting in synchronized rhythm, building into a hotter and hotter climax, until he came in one big shove into me, one big shove that shattered my G-spot, sending waves of body-numbing sensation all over my skin, flooding my brain with pure sensation, and I held him close and let myself feel. I felt it all, every last ounce, and I thought about nothing—nothing at all.

I felt skin on skin, sweat on sweat, body in body, and I felt like I'd finally been born.

* * *

I took a shower when I got home from work. As I often do, I scrutinized myself in the bathroom mirror while drying myself off. My skin was taut, my eyes clear, my hairline intact. I shifted my jaw to the right and then to the left—my German ancestry had left me with a well-defined jaw, and something else had left me with well-defined cheekbones. Those, combined with the white teeth, brown eyes, and my fastidiously maintained muscular build, gave me a feeling of well-being and satisfaction. Come what may, to my life or those around me, my body behaved exactly the way I needed it to. My arms, my shoulders—it was all perfect. Life might provide variables and uncertainties, but my body I could control. I smiled back at myself in acknowledgment of our private conversation, our private agreement to stick together. Still smiling, I left the bathroom and fixed myself a stiff martini.

The doorbell rang a short time later. I swallowed the last of my drink and went to answer the door. For a second, as I swung the door open, I didn't recognize her. There was little sign of the Lanie I'd met at work—this woman had a different energy, this woman was taller, leaner, stronger. I looked her up and down, registering the heels, the coat. Even the ponytail looked different. I couldn't tell exactly how, there was something different about her—but the eyes, with their careful mascara and perfect shadow, those were still Lanie's, and I grinned when I found them.

"Aren't you going to ask me in?" she asked, pushing her way past me.

So the little girl had some attitude tonight, was that it? I wondered if she'd already started drinking, or if this was just some new act she was trying to try to get me hot.

I stayed in the foyer, too distracted to shut the door properly, while I watched the act continue. Lanie stood in the foyer, her eyes looking at mine, her finger hovering over the zipper. She unzipped her coat down to her chest, halfway down her cleavage. It didn't look like she was wearing a bra. I wondered if she was wearing anything else under that long coat. I wondered why I'd never seen that coat before.

"Close the door. Come make me a drink."

Her words jolted me out of my daze, and I stepped forward into the living room. Damn right I'd make her a drink, I'd make her a nice strong drink, and we'd see what happened to her attitude then.

"What can I fix you?"

"Vodka. On the rocks."

Perfect. I'd get her trashed in no time. I poured her drink and made myself another martini. I turned to give her hers, but she grabbed it out of my hand and finished it off with one quick move. This was highly irregular. If there was one thing that was consistent about Lanie's drinking, it was that she nursed her drinks like a well-trained socialite. I wondered if something had happened that she hadn't told me about. I couldn't figure out what was going on.

She grinned at me. I'd never seen a grin quite like that on her—it was sort of naughty, sort of daring, and it was unlike her.

Totally unlike her. For once, I wasn't quite sure what my next move should be, and that was totally unlike me.

"I think it's time to get started."

What? Lanie calling the shots? What the hell was going on here?

"Finish your drink," she told me, pointing to my left hand.

Right. My drink. I'd almost forgotten about it, distracted as I was by the surreal aspect of the situation. I drank it down with impatience. This girl was starting to get on my nerves. Seemed like she was getting a little uppity for her own good. Seemed like she might need to be put back in her place, and my patience was running out.

Before I could make a move, she slid her right hand across her chest and pulled the zipper all the way down. I almost laughed. All the little drama queen needed was a spotlight. Somehow she'd decided her J.Crew sweaters weren't cutting it anymore. I wondered if she'd pulled this outfit out of the back of her closet— more secrets from a past she hadn't told me about—or if she'd bought her thigh-highs on the way home from work. I smiled to myself, thinking of little Lanie picking out those shoes in some kinky S&M store downtown. I wondered if she even knew where those stores were.

Leaning over to me, she put her mouth right next to my ear. "I want you to fuck me," she whispered. "I want you to fuck me," she said again, louder, sliding her hand around my back and pulled me close with a sudden motion. "Fuck me now."

I have to admit, laughable as the whole situation and her black wristbands were, my cock got hard. She was turning me on. Her little act, her breathy voice, her pathetically defiant attitude, it made me want to fuck her all the more. I wanted to slam her body against the wall, I wanted to see her underneath me while I rammed myself inside her, I wanted to mess up that makeup and that hair, I wanted to see her sweaty and panting, I wanted to shove myself so far into her that I split her in half.

She slipped her hand back around to my stomach, pushing me soundly against the wall. Ah, I see, the little cunt had a routine all worked out, a little dominatrix act that maybe she'd picked up watching late-night TV? With her hand pressed against my stomach, her eyes looking straight into mine—and I have to say, they looked fucking sexy with her heavy eyelashes and this new confrontational stare—she brought her lips next to mine, flicking her tongue over them before repeating, "Fuck me. I want you to fuck me."

I could barely stand it. My cock was pressing so hard against my pants, my body craving the way hers felt underneath me, my mind desperate to dominate her, but, with what self-control I had left, I pulled it together. I enjoyed the frustration, I was getting off on her little act, and I wanted to see where she went with it. I was going to let it go until I couldn't stand it anymore, then I was going to fuck her fucking brains out.

Tempting as always, she slowly moved her hand down my

stomach, over my pelvis, resting her hand over my dick. I was starting to lose patience. The feel of her hand on my cock was driving me crazy, and I couldn't keep my eyes off those stilettos. Why hadn't I seen those before tonight?

"Come on, Matt," she said, giving me her best Eartha Kitt impersonation. "Don't you have anything to say? Don't you want to fuck me?"

"Yes, yes, of course, I do." Time was ticking. My cock was growing more demanding. She didn't have a lot of time left before I reminded her who was in charge.

"Then let's get to it," she exclaimed, her hand grabbing my belt buckle as she pulled me into the bedroom.

I was more than ready for her. I quickly threw my clothes on the floor. She kept her heels and belt on because I was starting to like them. I was starting to get into seeing them on her. Her little show of strength made the prospect of dominating her all the more appealing.

She got on the bed, and I got on top of her. My cock between her legs, I was ready to turn the tables on this situation.

"Come on, I can't stand it," the bitch cried to me, and I smiled to myself. We'll see who's in charge now. She wrapped her feet around my waist as I pushed my way into her. Now this was more like it.

This was the way it should be. Just thinking of her little coat, of her prancing feet, of the cocky way she'd looked at me as I'd opened the door, thinking of the way she'd downed that vodka, the way she'd pressed me against the wall and pulled me to her— I was raging. I was hard. I wanted to fuck her until she broke in two. I wanted that attitude to be mine, I wanted her to be mine, I wanted my cock to find her hot wetness, I wanted that little bitch to cry for more, I wanted her to cry for me. That act was just an act—but this is where it got real, this is where I took charge.

And take charge I did, but she thrust back at me like a little lion. It made me want to eat her alive. She kicked her heels up, pressing her thighs at me—she'd never been like this in bed, and it made me twice as wired, twice as hard, twice as determined to shove my way through her act and through her desire, into that raw hot spot that my cock found when we were so wet and sweaty that nothing else mattered.

I kept going, sweat falling off my forehead, running down my arms, coating my thighs, my legs, her stomach, her breasts. There was no time for anything but fucking. We went harder and faster, her heels digging into my waist, pain irrelevant, my cock going deeper, again and again and again, filling her with my body, my balls pressed against her, pouring myself into her in a mad rush to get there, somewhere, anywhere—nothing existed but the rush of my cock and her sweaty moans, her hands clutching at me, and I went faster and faster until I came. There wasn't even time to pull out—I just came inside her, pressed so deep inside, that I don't know if I could have found my way out even if I'd wanted to.

I felt my breath heaving in my chest, I saw her breath heaving in hers, breasts moving up and down, their rhythm matching mine. My arms pressed down on the bed, damp with sweat, hers still wrapped around my waist. I stayed there for a while. I didn't want to leave. I wanted to do it all over again. I'd never felt like this before. I'd never thought I would, but now all I craved was her control.

James and Molly

He almost made me forget every boy I'd ever kissed. Almost, but not quite—of course. Because who can ever do that? But there was a moment there, a moment where for a second, I got lost in the thought of his tongue in my mouth, of my tongue waiting while his explored mine in a teasing, tender kind of way. Not lost in the thought, really, because in that second, I had stopped thinking. That's the point, after all. I had stopped thinking—about where I was, about who he was, about who might have come before . . .

That was only for a second, though, when my brain obligingly turned off to let me lose myself in the sensation, but then it slipped back on to remind me that I was a bit fat, and where did I want him to touch me, and where didn't I want him to touch me, and did I really like him, anyway, and what did he look like again (because you know once the lights are off and you're a little drunk, you do forget), and how had we met?

Who had come before was a question toward which I resisted letting my brain wander, since that would involve real thinking. While it was easy enough to remember the big ones, the Relationships or the Affairs, there was still that blond boy who had done it to me so well kneeling down on the floor while I lay on the bed but whose name has been lost to the hands of time (and whom I'd sort of let slip away precisely because of that terrible tattoo on his hands), or that guy who had been on the television show and who had bartended at that place in the West Village and who never called me again, but who wasn't really good anyway (and so somehow my brain had cooperated by forgetting his name), and the one who got me back to his place by telling me he wanted to show me his new stereo, but then I didn't even end up hearing anything on it because the sex sort of happened (and I went along with it because it was easier than making a scene), then, a year or two later, he ended up marrying one of my friends.

There were those three, and the others, of course, whose personal details would only be found through prolonged effort or hypnosis, those people who slip through your life like water, both under your skin in a moment (moments?) of intimacy and warmth but gone before you can get a grip—one of those symptoms of living in a big city where so many people are crowded together and still alone.

But this was not the time to think about this, so I stood up to my brain and shoved the nag aside, trying to enjoy the feeling of his body against mine, his tongue with mine, the softness of his lips—slow motion, soft focus, just like in the movies.

The movies. Yes, that's kind of how we met.

It felt like a moment out of *Less than Zero*, except that *Less than Zero* was in LA, and I'd just gotten out of the taxi in St. Tropez. Still, there was something about the way everyone was eating lunch with their sunglasses on, at the table by the pool, while I still had on my winter clothes from the plane, my bulky sleeping bag of coat and my hat, while they sat in the sun and looked at me as I came around the corner of the house, all turning to make me remember the holes in my coat where little bits of down poked through, and I felt like someone caught wearing off-the-rack at a Versace show, like Molly Ringwald in the first half of a John Hughes movie, before anyone has discovered how lovely she really is.

He didn't turn to stare at me, though. He stayed with his back to me, looking down at his food, while I quickly pushed my suitcase into a corner, dumped my coat and hat on top of it, and tried somehow to slip into a chair with the minimal amount of attention and introductions.

It was only when I was sitting down, when I had pulled my

chair close to the table and was trying to sort out what food, exactly, was still left and still available, that I was able to look at him out of the corner of my eye.

And that was when I thought of James Spader, and wondered if any of John Hughes's movies had been set in LA and who directed *Less than Zero,* anyway?

But back to James. Who didn't have a crush on him? I mean, not now, of course, but then? Back then when he was slick and cool and bad in that way that was so very, very good? Oh, James Spader in *Less than Zero.* I would have married him in a heartbeat. I would have done things to him in an LA sports car that would have made anyone forget Jami Gertz. I would have—

Mr. Spader looked up at me and nodded. I nodded back.

"Hi, I'm Sarah."

"Michael."

I nodded again. Where does one go after that? It's not exactly a great conversation opener—not to mention the fact that he seemed a bit like he was in pain, although that could just have been because he was squinting into the sun.

If he'd really been James Spader, he'd have had sunglasses.

I thought about that and watched him out of the corner of my eye while helping myself to the odd bits of food that had survived the lunch. I ate a cauliflower floret and studied his nose. He really was good-looking. Despite the squinting, his eyes were a clear blue, his nose well-defined, straight and nicely sized. His jaw German. His hair blond. He actually kind of looked a bit like me if I'd been a business-y type of man, or if I'd learned to affect a surly elegance.

Lunch was over before I'd had a chance to think of what to say next. He was off into town with some of the others, and I was off to my room to unpack and catch my breath, being very sure to register that his room was the one next door to mine.

I didn't see him again until just before dinner.

I can't remember what I was doing, but I was doing something because when there was a knock at the door, I was totally unprepared. It's amazing how many times you wait for a knock and there's nothing, then when you're in the middle of something— that's when someone drops by.

So I was in the middle of something, and there was a knock, and suddenly my small room went from having one person in it to having three, and it was Laura and Michael, and they had come to fetch me for dinner.

Only Laura was wearing a short stylish black-and-white number, and Michael had on a tie, so I said, give me two minutes, and while Michael rolled a joint, I made myself pretty.

A funny thing about me is that I clean up well. I'm remarkably capable of looking bland and incongruous, and I'm quite happy to spend days in my sweatpants, but give me two minutes, the right dress, and a bit of makeup, and I can be a superstar—or at least look like one.

So it was with a fair amount of pleasure that I darted into the bathroom, heels and dress in hand, ignoring the conversation Michael and Laura were having in the corner, to clean myself up.

Wow, Laura exclaimed, when I reemerged, but I was less concerned with that than with Michael's double take. I smiled to myself. We'd begun to play.

Several glasses of champagne later, and a tableful of French food, we were somewhere in "downtown" St. Tropez—if there is such a thing. The club was called Provacateur. The music was hard, fast, a bit electro, but no one was dancing. I didn't care. They had a pole.

I could feel the music pumping through my head and my hips, and I could feel Michael watching me. I could feel myself watching him. I wanted to have sex with his cheekbones, and I knew I could make him want to have sex with my legs.

Boom, boom, boom. Lights. Music. Beats. Alcohol. Third bottle of champagne? Fourth? I couldn't keep track, and I couldn't stop dancing. I might have had doubts about my conversational skills, I might have been insecure about my manners or my etiquette, and my French didn't go much beyond kissing, but I knew what to do with a pole. Stripping had taught me that much.

I made my way around it. Up it. Against it. I ran it between my legs. I bent backward. Forward. Left, right. Right, left. Boom, boom, boom. Lights. Music. Beats. Alcohol. Michael was watching me. I was watching him. Laura and the others were still there, but I barely saw them. It was all about the action. It was all about my plans. It was all about what I wanted and what I would make him want.

And that was me.

I watched him get up from the booth and head, a bit drunkenly, to the bathroom. I waited a minute, and then I slipped off the dance floor.

He almost didn't see me as he walked past.

"Michael."

"Sarah. Hello."

"D'you know where the bathroom is?"

"Yeah, sure, it's just over there."

"Over where?"

"Back behind the bar, to your right."

"Can you show me?"

Without waiting for a response, I took his hand and pulled him in the direction of the bar.

"It's just aro—"

I ignored him and made him follow me into the small room. I locked the door. I looked at him. He looked at me. Alcohol had made him weak and me strong.

"Michael."

He looked at me. I looked at him. And then I kissed him. I pressed myself up against him, which pressed him up against the door, and my lips against his. I wanted to feel his body against mine, his heat, his strength, the slim sleekness of his body, and I wanted his hands against my back.

He seemed to know enough to put them there.

I kissed him. I felt him against me. I could feel him getting hard. I could hear the music through the bathroom door. The lights, the heat, the beats, the sweat—it was a *Less than Zero* moment, and I loved it. Drunk on champagne, in the thick of it all, he was James Spader, and I was anyone but myself.

I ran my hand down his chest, across his stomach, and between his legs. He was hard. He felt like a fucking telephone. I grabbed him. He moaned.

"Oh, it's beautiful," I whispered.

"Touch it," he begged.

"Later," I said.

"Now?"

"Later."

"Please . . . ?"

"Okay." I relented. It would just make him want it more—later.

I got down on my knees and unzipped his pants. He wanted me so much, it was amazing. I let him slip out between the opening in his boxers. Smooth, pink, and hard. I smiled to myself. The whole situation was completely surreal. There was nothing about this that felt like real life.

I ran my tongue along the edge of his cock. One lick, two licks, three licks, four—then I stood up.

"That's it, darling. The rest you'll have to get later . . . if you're a good boy, that is."

I gave him one more kiss and left him in the bathroom to pull himself together.

I don't know exactly what time we got back to our rooms. It was somewhere after three and before five. I just remember all of us in Laura's room, finishing her minibar's champagne, smoking some joints as fast as we could roll them, and lying on Laura's bed with her and Michael. I remember being hyperaware of his legs against mine and the way his hand was draped across my hip. I remember taking every opportunity to shift my body closer to his. I remember wondering if he was doing the same or if he was too drunk to pay attention to such finesse.

And then it suddenly got late, and the others got up to go back to their room, and we all sort of collectively gathered our things, and then the others were gone, and then Michael and I said good night to Laura and walked past the pool toward our adjacent rooms.

All that was a blur, because I only started really registering when Michael asked if I wanted one more glass of champagne in his room.

I would have said that my brain snapped awake at that point, but I kind of liked the combination of heady champagne swirl and being a bit stoned, and I figured anything that helped take the edge off the panic was a good thing. So I kept my brain moving on autopilot while I smiled and said, a glass of champagne would be lovely, thanks.

If I kept my brain just slightly on, I could just slightly forget who I was, and accept that it was totally normal and okay that I was at this hotel in the south of France, about to have yet another glass of champagne with a man who looked like James Spader and probably had the same size bank account. And if I kept all that going, then maybe, just maybe, I'd let myself go enough to let him put his hand down my pants, and maybe I'd be able to keep feeling strong enough to put my hand down his.

And so it went, oh blessed champagne.

We sat side by side on the edge of his bed, and we talked. I couldn't possibly say what we talked about, because I wasn't really paying attention. I drank slowly, feeling the bubbles in my mouth match the butterflies in my stomach. I watched his mouth move and thought about what it would be like to kiss it again. I watched his eyes watching me and tried to read his mind.

"Or I could just kiss you," he said.

I don't know what happened before, but I know what happened after. He leaned over and kissed me. He kissed me, and I kissed him back, and it was wonderful and marvelous, and I dropped my (empty) glass somewhere on the bed, and I pulled myself up and fell on top of him, his back to the mattress, my chest against his, his arms around my stomach, and we kissed. Hard.

Just like in the movies.

The bed was enormous, and we used every inch of it. He took my shirt off first, but then his came off before my bra. My skirt stayed on, but my underwear ended up on the floor. I don't know how drunk he was, but he had every bit of coordination that I could have hoped for. He almost made me forget every boy I'd ever kissed. He almost made me forget what it had been like to have my breasts kissed, my skin stroked, my body fucked. It didn't feel like it was really me there, anyway, so maybe it was the first time for whoever I was.

And, whoever I was, I started off on top. I straddled him, watching him watch my body, and somehow not worrying about the imperfections, not caring that the room was still lit and he could see me, all of me, while I took off my bra, slowly, holding it up with one arm while unhooking it with the opposite hand. I tossed it aside and took his hands, placing them over my breasts, looking into his eyes while he touched me, caressed me, fondled me.

Keeping my eyes on his, I reached down to unbutton his pants, leaning forward to meet his lips while I lay on top of him, my weight against his, feeling the sensation of his flesh on mine. I wanted to go slow, I wanted to savor every minute, I wanted to remember every delicious second—and knowing that I was going to get what I wanted, I knew how wonderful the anticipation could be.

He wrapped his arms around me, pulling me close, one hand roaming up and down my back, the other sliding up my neck to cradle the back of my head. As he kissed me, he rolled us over so that suddenly he was on top, I was on bottom, his body pressing mine against his, into the bed. I could feel him between my legs, I could feel him everywhere.

He took both of my hands in his, gently holding them at first, then dragging them above my head, pulling them together, grasping both of my wrists in one of his hands. I struggled at first, more for show than for purpose, but I didn't stand much of a chance, anyway—and I wanted it all as much as he did.

He slid one muscular thigh between my legs, pressing against me as he kissed down my neck and across my chest. He kissed my upper chest and my collarbone. He kissed my left shoulder and my right. He kissed my skin—while, at the same time, his other hand was sliding its way across my breasts and down my stomach.

As I arched against him, begging him with my body to put his hand between my legs, he only made it worse by teasing my nipples with his lips and teeth—then, just to render me entirely useless, just to tease me more, and maybe even to tease himself, he slipped his hand between my legs.

My skirt was still on, but I knew the fabric was wet. I could feel his hand across the front of my thigh, between my legs, grazing the inside of my thigh with his fingertips, brushing against my clit and every inch of skin that craved for more. Oh my god, put your hand inside me, I wanted to shout—but I bit my lip and waited to see what he would do next.

He released my hands, running his second hand across my wrist, down my arm, and over my breasts. I turned toward him.

"I want you inside me," I whisper, but so quietly he can't hear.

"What?" He moves his head closer to my mouth.

"I want you inside me," I whisper again, but this time he hears me.

"Now? Or later?" He grins.

"Now, now, now. Oh, please. Now."

I reached down and undid my skirt. He reached down and zipped it back.

"Leave it on. I like it."

I stared at him for a minute, at his blue eyes looking at my blue eyes, then I ran my fingers down his body, across his chest, down his stomach, feeling his stomach muscles twitch as I ran over them. I leaned over, running my tongue across his chest . . . he tasted delicious, a combination of sweat and skin and desire.

I grabbed his nipple in my mouth and bit down, causing him to take a deep, quick breath, running my tongue across his flesh, while my hands continued to feel every inch of his body that they could reach—including his gloriously hard cock. I slid my hand up and down its length, pausing at the base, giving him a squeeze, then sliding my hand down between his legs, gently cupping his balls. He arched up to meet me, and I turned to meet him. I shifted my legs just so, and he slid right in.

And then I called him James.

He stopped what he was doing (which involved being inside

me while his tongue licked my left breast) and looked at me with a confused expression.

I laughed. I explained. I told him the whole story. I told him about the movie and the sunglasses and the lunch. I told him about my insecurities, and my eighties movie obsession, and how I used to be a stripper, and how I liked it because I could be someone else, and how sometimes pretending I was Molly Ringwald made me feel like, by the end of the movie, someone would discover how beautiful I really was. And how I was really painfully shy and how it made it easier for me, somehow, to have sex with people if I felt like I was in the movies, and not me, or if I was doing it for money, rather than for love, because then it felt safer, somehow.

I probably wouldn't have told him so much if it wasn't so late and I hadn't been so drunk, and maybe he wouldn't have listened so well if he'd had somewhere else to be or if he hadn't been so drunk. I don't know. There's no way to tell. But he listened to everything I said, his eyes on mine, his hands around my hips, and it was so easy to talk to him, so I told him everything.

"So if you do it for money," he asked, "it's safer?"

"Yes. Somehow. Love can hurt. Money makes it easier."

"And if it's not really you, then you can enjoy it more?"

"Yes. Somehow. I'm sorry I can't explain better."

"No, no, that's okay." He thought for a minute, his blue eyes on mine. I started to wonder if I'd said too much.

"So, Molly," he said, a grin snaking its way across his face, "if

I pay you to have sex with me, you think you might let yourself fall in love?"

I blinked.

"You can call me James."

I grinned. This was crazy. Who was this guy?

"All I want to do is see you again. And I don't mind playing games. Do we have a deal, Molly?"

I nodded. It was bizarre, but when had that stopped me before? There was a moment of silence while we looked at each other.

"All right, Molly, I think it's later, now. What do you think?"

I nodded. "You're right, James. It's definitely later."

And with that, the games officially began.

Deep House

The room was full of fashion week refugees, their expensively distressed jeans flaring over their viciously pointed stilettos, their skimpy halter tops cut to expose perfectly toned arms and abs. Without the requisite clutch or matching shoes, it seemed painfully obvious that I was crashing this particular party.

Instead, I wore this really supershort red leather miniskirt I have that wraps around and fastens with little snaps. It sits low on my hips and just barely covers my ass, maybe you remember it? On my legs were black thigh-high socks with black high-heeled boots and a black tank top with skinny little straps that I safety-pinned on the sides so that it gathered a bit to expose just a tiny bit of skin on either side of my stomach, right above the edge of the skirt. On top, I wore a tight black sweater with white stripes on the sleeve that zips up the front—but that didn't stay on too long once I started dancing. Underneath the skirt I wore my low-cut black satin underwear, but no one could see that . . .

There is something about the bass in house music that totally gets under my skin, and I could feel it warming me and filling me up and making me completely wet on that dance floor while I kept thinking how much I wished you were there, so that I could put my arms around you and pull you in and kiss you and feel your chest against my head, your arm around my back, your hand against my spine.

But you weren't there. Instead I was dancing with Nick, whose British accent charmed me while his offerings of white wine loosened me enough to flirt properly. It took me two glasses to get onto the dance floor, but, once I did, I didn't leave. I kept dancing, feeling more and more confident as the beats grew tighter, and the night grew longer.

When Nick and I first made our way to the lower level set between two massive speakers, I could barely make eye contact. I felt the wine seeping its way into my bloodstream as the bass pounded through my skin and into my head. The more the wine seeped and the bass pounded, the more relaxed I got, and the more space I took up on the dance floor.

Still avoiding eye contact, which I could tell Nick was trying steadily to attain, I leaned over: "Their manicures cost more than I spend on food."

"They need to spend that much," he said. "You don't."

Instantly satisfied, I rewarded Nick with eye contact and a slow stroke on the arm—then back to dancing.

Few men can dance well, and Nick was no exception to that rule. He did what I'd call a boogie, shaking his arms about, looking sort of goofy and very white. I stopped watching and slipped back into my world. The speakers were incredible, and if I let myself go, I could feel the sound washing over me. I kept dancing, ignoring the people around me, just feeling the beat move my legs and my arms, knowing that Nick was watching me as I watched no one.

It felt like the coldest night of the winter, and every time someone entered the club, the draft whisked its way through the crowd. In a popular club on a popular night, the drafts never really stop coming, but the longer I danced, the hotter I got, until I could gradually unzip my sweater. Even though I didn't really need to take it off, I started by just opening it all the way, knowing that my movements would reveal just enough shoulder to keep Nick's eyes still focused on me.

I decided to practice the gradual stripper technique—first shoulder. Then other shoulder. Then both shoulders. Then sweater off. I tied it around my waist and kept moving. The deep house beats continued relentlessly as the lights seemed to dim. Almost without me noticing, the lights had receded to a rosy glow, supplemented by the subtle red lights that lined the walls. The club's walls were covered with long cylindrical rows of padding that created the feel of a very soft, very warm log cabin. We, in the center of the room, dancing away under a spinning disco ball, were in our very own Swiss chalet.

The sweater off—bra strap alternately up, then down—I made sure to turn around, letting him check out my tattoo, before turning back again to make sure he noticed my breasts, accentuated by the combination of low-cut top and push-up bra. I still avoided the eye contact, but I didn't have to look at him to know he was staring.

I kept dancing, watching the bodies around me, watching the couples on every side, wishing that I could take this maneuver one step further and feel the actual touch of arms around me. The combination of the heat, the pulsing bass, the dancing, the people, in the middle of this Swiss chalet in the middle of New York's West Village, made me desperately want to press my lips against someone's, to thrust myself against him as he thrust himself against me, to feel his arms around my waist, reaching under my shirt and up my skirt, pulling every inch of me close to every inch of him, feeling the warmth of his taste within the warmth of mine, tongues and teeth and lips and skin combining.

But all I did was wish for it, for the sweaty heat of it, and avoid eye contact while dancing, dancing, dancing.

The beats kept pulsing onward, the night ticked on, and we all kept moving. Nick's friends—a product manager at a record label and a musician—joined us on the dance floor. I looked up, smiling at them, and turned my eyes back to the floor.

Thump. Thump. Thump. I could feel the couples intertwining around me, the lateness of the hour and the consumption of the alcohol creating a heady mix where makeup was forgotten and hair got messy. Those of us on the dance floor only cared about the beat, about moving our legs and our arms, shaking our hips and making more heat.

The ones outside the dance floor? We barely noticed them. This club had a lowered dance floor, a couple of steps beneath the rest of the room, which created even more of an illusion that we were all partners in a hedonistic ritual, and the rest were just voyeurs, standing there, drinks in hand, permanent grins on their faces, laughing, talking, air-kissing.

We couldn't hear them, and we barely saw them. We kept dancing.

I could feel Nick watching me, and I used that gaze to boost the bass, to move even faster, to lift my arms and stamp my feet. I let the wine blur the line between me and the music. I let Nick's gaze blur the line between me and the person I wanted to become.

I kept dancing.

Nick continued with his white-man boogie, but I barely noticed. All I needed from him was to be watched. The rest was up to me.

I felt an arm on my back. I turned to see that Nick had stopped dancing.

Sweaty, exuberant, hot with sex, I smiled at him, looked him in the eyes, and kept dancing. He leaned over and pressed his face against my ear to ask if I liked the club.

I replied, leaning back over to him, pressing my chest against his arm, that I thought it was great, I just wished more people were making out.

It was true—all the discotequers were dancing in one big throbbing mass, lit by the warm glow, unified by the structure of the beat—but no one seemed to feel the sexual urgency that was overwhelming me. This music made me want to fuck, but it just seemed to make them want to lift their glasses higher and shake their hair.

Nick grinned back at me, suggesting that maybe I should lead by example.

I looked at him, straight in the eyes. I held that eye contact for the first time all night, staring straight at the brilliant blue circles that were staring straight back into mine.

"Are you saying you want to make out with me?"

The world seemed to stop there, or at least the music dropped out and the disco ball stopped turning, and Nick confessed that he'd wanted to all night.

Each word dropped into my head, slipping past my earlobe, into my ear canal, rushing its way past my brain, around my heart, through my gut, straight down to the space between my legs. I felt the warmth, the wetness explode, as I pulled him to me and pushed my tongue between his lips. I felt the warmth of his mouth, the taste of his tongue running along the inside of my teeth, the sheer solidness of his chest pressed up against the sweaty softness of mine. I let myself fall into him as the music surged back, louder and more impatient than ever.

And then he pulled back.

Off-balance, I looked at him, mouth caught in midpause.

"Not here," he said.

Those words dropped like the last ones, only these were an entirely different breed—these words were cold and icy and came accompanied with steel weights that grabbed hold and yanked everything down, down, down.

I didn't let that stop me. I was ready to go.

I smiled back at him, matching blue eyes with blue eyes, as I asked him to find me someone else then.

"Absolutely not," he replied, blue eyes forced to crinkle by the smile underneath.

I kept dancing, staring straight at him, knowing he couldn't stop staring back. I waited to see what he'd say next as I began to scout the room for another willing body.

He asked me if we could find a quiet room, a question that had a million connotations, but only two answers.

"Sure. Where?"

"There isn't really anything here . . ." He gestured around the pulsing red walls of our Swiss chalet disco.

I thought about that. I knew where he lived and, although I didn't think I could say no to much of anything, I could still say no to Brooklyn.

"How about my place?" I said.

Another blue-crinkling grin. "Deal. Let's go."

I went. All I wanted was to feel my tongue back in his mouth, to feel someone's arms reaching under my shirt, to feel the heady rush of messy physical touch again, so I grabbed my coat and walked with Nick into the nearest cab.

I thought of you as he held the door for me, and I tumbled in. The wind was icy cold, but I hadn't bothered to fasten my coat all the way. I was still full of heat. Nick slid into the cab behind me and slid his hand right under the coat, opening up the few snaps I had closed. My warm flesh quickly absorbed the shock of his cold hand and turned it hot. I told the driver my address, barely able to focus as Nick's hand reached around, behind my spine and down the curve of my waist. Directions provided, I turned back to Nick, air somehow escaping my lungs as I fell into his mouth. His tongue curled around mine as both his hands curled around my hips, pulling me onto his lap and up against him.

The frigid air seeped around the edge of the window, little droplets of condensation forming, but I barely noticed as I got lost in the heat emanating from between Nick's legs and from his mouth. We could barely stop to breathe. Nick's hands pressed against my legs, the tip of his middle finger hesitating on the outer edge of my panties, the other hand gripping my thigh. He traced the satin line that separated him from me, back and forth, back and forth. I pulled my head away and opened my eyes to find him staring at me. I smiled at him and ran my tongue over his lips. That was all the reassurance he needed—his fingers clenched around my thigh before running up, then down into my panties.

I could feel the firmness of his fingers pressing into me, sliding into the warm wetness that had craved being filled all night. I leaned back, sliding my hips forward, letting him touch every side of me, making his fingers go farther and deeper, as I grew wetter and hotter. His tongue licked my neck, his damp heat echoing mine. Barely able to stand it, I pushed my tongue into his mouth as I shoved my hips even closer to his, feeling his hot hardness pressed against my thigh. He slipped his fingers out, running their sticky wetness along my spine before pulling me tightly to him, my legs on either side of his waist, my damp underwear against his crotch, our tongues intertwined.

I unzipped his pants and rolled my hand over his underwear. His cock was hard, and I wrapped my fingers around him for a second, just holding, enjoying the warmth and thickness as they sent tingles up my back. He unbuttoned the top of his pants while looking into the front seat of the cab. We were almost at my apartment, we were running out of time. His pants open, I could see the outline of his cock, the head slipping over the waistline. I couldn't resist running my fingers across his exposed head. It was wet, a clear string of precum connecting my finger to his cock. I brought my finger up toward my mouth, the string illuminated by the flashing streetlights. It broke just as my finger reached my lips. I took his hand and wrapped my fingers around his, licking both, his taste mingling with mine, as the cab lurched to a stop.

I was just getting started, and it was clear he was, too. The cab driver tapped the window, and I looked at Nick. He glanced at me, then turned his head to the front of the car: "I'll give you a twenty to keep driving."

The cabbie shook his head and sighed, but it was too late and too cold to be turning down an offer like that. He pressed his foot back onto the accelerator as I pressed my hand back down Nick's pants. Nick gave a huge sigh while leaning his head back against the seat, and I started to rub. My fingers wrapped around his cock, I moved them up and down, gently but firmly shifting the skin back and forth. He got harder, and I could feel the veins filling with blood as I moved faster and tighter. I could see the precum glistening on the tip of his cock while I kept picking up speed, mixing shallow with deep—five deep, five shallow, five deep, five shallow, listening to his breath accelerate, feeling his thighs clench, his cock virtually thrusting itself into my hands.

Smiling to myself, I watched him lie back on the seat, pants unzipped, coat open, prostrate before me, entire body focused on my every motion. I felt my wetness seeping out from between my legs, an electric energy filling my thighs and pussy. He was practically panting now, one of his hands grabbing the door beside him. I leaned over and, without stopping my hand, very gently licked the precum off the tip of his cock. He moaned and shivered, ever so slightly. I slowed my fingers down but still kept my hand firmly clenched around his cock and began to run my tongue along the edge of it, down to the base and up around the head. Nick moaned again as the cab kept driving down Avenue B. The time had come.

I circled the end of his cock with my lips and closed tight. I sucked my way down to the base of his cock, pushing the skin back with my hand, and started running my tongue up and down, back and forth. I could feel his thighs clench tighter. I started to work. I began moving my head along with the rhythm of his breathing, releasing my lips when I got the base of his cock, tightening them again at the tip. Every time I got to the tip, I allowed my tongue a quick circuit around the ridge, before plunging back down to the base, sending my tongue to follow along the main vein. I knew he was about to explode.

I gradually picked up the pace, faster and faster, keeping my lips tight and my grip hard. He started to shiver noticeably, his feet twitching, his right hand clenching the edge of the door, his left hand clenching the edge of the seat. I stole a glance up at him—his eyes were closed, his head back against the leather. I watched his face grow tight; he was almost there.

I relaxed my lips and intensifed the grip of my hand around his cock, letting the movement grow a bit more shallow as I picked up even more speed.

And then, with a huge sigh and a perfectly coordinated effort, his cum shot into my mouth, his fingers released their grip, his thighs relaxed, and his feet stopped moving. I paused—feeling the last lingering spasms—running my tongue very gently across the tip of his cock, licking up the remaining bits of cum, before pulling myself back up onto the seat.

Running my hand over my mouth, I wiped off the mixture of spit and cum and sweat. He pulled me to him and ran his tongue into mine, wrapping his arms around my waist and holding me tight. I could feel him trying to catch his breath. I lay against him, his chest heaving, body relaxed and warm. I enjoyed his warmth, but I enjoyed even more the electric energy I still felt.

Slipping off his lap, I leaned back against the cab door and slowly spread my legs. Staring straight into his eyes, watching him watch me, I licked the tips of my fingers, then, now covered with his cum and my saliva, slid them around the edge of my underwear and straight into my wet and aching pussy. With a sigh of relief, I shoved my first two fingers inside as far as they'd go, feeling them curve along the edge of my body, pressing the hot flesh of my insides, running them along the soft skin. I shoved them in and out, slowly, just enough to make me start to leak.

He saw my wetness seeping out of my pussy and reached over with his hand to run his fingers through it.

Shaking my head, I took my left high-heeled boot and pressed him straight in the chest with it. He stared at me, confused, a slight grin at the edge of his mouth, as though this were a game. I pressed harder and shook my head again. I used my knee to knock his hand against the edge of the seat and, while holding it there and holding his gaze in mine, I licked the tips of my fingers again and, once more, slid them inside me—first one, then two. While holding the two in there and gently moving them in and out, I started rubbing my clitoris in steady circles with my thumb.

I kept his hand pressed to the edge of the seat with my knee, and, the more I rubbed, the harder I pushed my left boot against his chest. All he could do was watch. My nipples started to get harder under my shirt, so I reached my left hand behind my bra and began rubbing them, first one, then the other, and, as I pinched them, ever so slightly, they grew harder and redder. Nick's face began turning red as well, and I could see his cock getting hard again, little droplets of precum starting to form along the tip. He could tell I was staring at it, and, the more I stared, the harder he got.

My face starting to flush, my nipples looked as hard as his cock and my clitoris as swollen. I took my fingers out of my pussy and, sliding back in the seat so that my boot now rested on his shoulder and my head against the door, I started rubbing my clit in earnest—round and round and round—so swollen it was almost painful but the most electrifying delicious pain. My eyes closed as I could feel myself getting closer, the sensation building.

I started to come, tingling in every inch of me, and I kept rubbing, circles and circles, pinching my left nipple tighter and tighter, my boot shoving him against the opposite door, my left knee still pressing his hand against the seat, rubbing and pinching and panting until the rush threatened to make me explode, and still I kept going—then I exploded, into a warm perfect flood of euphoric bliss that filled me from toe to toe, finger to finger, breast to breast.

Lying back against the door, I let my right hand hang down between my legs, my left hand cupping my aching tit, my right knee still pressed against his hand, my left boot now resting in his lap, just barely touching his rigid cock. As I caught my breath, I delicately prodded him with my boot, watching his cock move from side to side, the precum leaking onto the seat.

Almost home, the cab was heading down Avenue B for the fifth time that night. I pulled my underwear back into place and snapped my coat shut.

With some effort, he shoved his cock back into his underwear and zipped his pants. As he started to close his coat up, I shook my head: "It'll be better if I go now."

Nick looked at me, startled, again as though this were a game. I touched his fingers with my hand, halting their progress as they fastened buttons.

I ran my wet fingers around the edge of his mouth, my fluids mixing with his, then leaned over to give him one more kiss. I licked his teeth with my tongue as he tried to pull me to him. I pulled back, gave him one more quick kiss on the lips, and asked the driver to stop.

Flustered, still trying to close his coat, Nick asked a bit desperately if I wanted to get coffee or a drink.

I shook my head and told him I had to get some sleep. One more quick chaste kiss, then I grabbed my gloves and hat, sliding out the door. As I hurried up the stairs to my apartment, all I could think about was getting into bed, where I could replay the night's events—only this time the fantasy would be all about you.

The Gift

The martinis were stronger than they should be before four o'clock, and lunch took twice as long, but it was my birthday, so I didn't really care. I've always been pretty good at not letting on how drunk I felt, and today was no different. Making my way back to my desk, a neat grin on my face, my feet methodically moving left, right, left, right in my pointy black patent leather heels, I slid gratefully into my seat and exhaled slowly.

All I had to do was keep staring at my monitor for a couple more hours and I could leave early. All I had to do was stare and type a few words and no one would know that I was wasted off my ass. I just had to keep my mouth shut, my face focused, and no one would know the difference.

"Rachel?"

I turned around.

"Um, someone left this at the front desk for you."

Michael reached forward and gently placed an artfully wrapped package on top of TO BE FILED. I stared. I knew this package would impress me even if I wasn't seeing double—the bow was red luscious silk, the paper was as smooth as satin and as brilliantly red as my fingernails, and the box was big enough to cover my entire desk.

"Do you know who dropped this off?" I asked, turning around, but Michael had already gone back to the mailing room, leaving me alone with my oversize gift.

I glanced around the room, but no one seemed to have any interest in me or my enormous red box. I debated for a second whether to open it now or save it for later, but knew that I couldn't resist, and so, with a sigh and a tingle of anticipation, I delicately slipped the bow off and ran my nails under the tape keeping the paper shut. With a satisfying hiss, the wrapping fell to the sides, and I stared at the white cardboard box.

I looked once more at the wrapping paper—no note, no explanation. Having no idea who would give me such a large present, much less deliver it to my desk, I opened up the box and peered inside, hoping the contents would provide some answers.

At first, all I saw was a neatly folded stack of black lace, underwire, and red ribbon. I looked around the room—no one was watching. Was this some kind of joke? Without taking the fabric out of the box, I reached in and lifted up the material. I groped with my left hand to see if there was anything underneath. My fingers found a slim metal chain—and nothing else.

What the fuck? I looked around the room again, but no one was watching, no one was snickering, no one was paying me any attention. Time to figure this one out, I thought. With a quick sudden motion, I slid the fabric out of the box and into my briefcase. As I stood up, I reached into the box one last time, grabbed the chain, and dropped it into my suit pocket, before making my way, calmly and professionally, to the restroom, all traces of inebriation eradicated by curiosity and adrenaline.

The bathroom door securely locked, I placed my briefcase on the shut toilet seat and opened it. The pile of lace and ribbon eyed me suggestively. I shook my head, smiling to myself—this was definitely the most intriguing birthday present I'd ever received. Lifting up the fabric, it took form, and I laughed out loud. Barely enough material to cover anything worth covering, I knew it would cover enough to make anyone lucky enough to see desperate to know what was underneath—and I knew it was the perfect size.

Within a matter of moments, my suit hung neatly on the hook behind the door, and I was wearing a decadent mass of material— all crisscrossed and tied and finessed around my breasts—the underwire fitting perfectly under my cleavage, the ribbon wrapped around my waist and lacing up the back of the corset, the red silk creating a pattern of X's against the sheer black lace of the rest of the garment. The box had also thoughtfully contained a pair of black thigh-highs topped off with an inch of red lace.

I didn't dare leave the stall to look at myself in the mirror for fear someone would walk in, but I didn't need to—I knew it fit me perfectly. Slipping on my heels, I leaned back and closed my eyes. Running my finger against the ribbon's smooth satin, I tried to remember how long it had been since someone had stroked me the same way. It had been a very long time.

My last boyfriend and I had split up almost a year earlier and between my work schedule and my distaste for bars and one-night stands, I'd slept alone every night since, which made this gift all the more mysterious. No one had shown much interest in me in a while, and the only appointments I made these days were with coworkers and clients.

As I ran my fingers back and forth over the trail of red ribbon, eyes closed, breath quickening, I let my mind wander.

By the time my fingers reached between my legs, I was all wet. With a rush of need and desire, I shoved first one, then two, inside, pressing along the curve of my body, breathing deeply as every inch of me focused on the hot wetness of my insides. I slowly started to push them in and out, my left hand making its way along the fine bone of the corset's underwire, cupping my breast and pinching my swollen nipple between my fingers.

The pain from my nipple, combined with the swelling of my clit and the pressure of my fingers, following a martini lunch, almost made me pass out. I slid back against the wall of the stall, falling into the corner, sweat glistening on my face, my hair in my eyes, as I pressed in and out, harder and faster, feeling every inch tighten, every inch beg for more, my clit craving the pressure of my fingers, my pussy craving the pressure of a cock. I alternated as quickly as I could—a few seconds outside, a few seconds inside, my fingers darting across the edge of my clit, back and forth, round and round, and then inside—quick, as deep and as hard as I could shove. In and out, round and round, back and forth, every motion of my right hand echoed by my left across my breasts.

Both breasts had long since been liberated from their lacy confines, and they swung over the underwire, quivering as my hips thrust forward and my entire body began to shake. I could feel myself starting to come—the hint of delicious pleasure teasing me on the edge of my horizons, a promise of what would come if I kept at it, if I didn't let up, if I shoved harder and deeper, if I pinched stronger and tighter, if my fingers moved faster and my hips pushed farther.

Leaning against that damn bathroom wall, my hair around my shoulders, my breath heavy, my face flushed, my wetness leaking down my thighs, I kept moving—my fingers, my hands, my hips, until I could feel the sensation building and building and building and—with one big rush, I exhaled as millions of tingling sensations rushed through me.

A huge grin on my face, I shoved my briefcase off the toilet and sat down. My chest was heaving, my head was spinning—and I felt amazing. I couldn't remember the last time I'd masturbated, and I certainly couldn't remember the last time I'd done it in a public restroom. It had been way too long. What a birthday present.

Ever since David had left, I'd gone into autopilot. Getting close to someone else seemed like way too much work and way too much risk. It was easier to focus on my friends and my job and my apartment. Without anyone to run their hand between my legs, without being woken up in the morning by someone pressing up against me, it was easy to forget that my body served anything but clinical purposes.

The last ten minutes had been a delicious reminder.

With my clit still throbbing and my nipples still swollen, I unhooked my corset and stepped back into my suit. I'd almost forgotten the day wasn't over. I looked at my watch—an hour or so until I could leave without guilt. I bent down to pick up my briefcase when a loud clang startled me out of my daze. I glanced over to see a pile of silver chain against the edge of the toilet.

I smiled to myself. I'd totally forgotten. What the hell was that? Reaching over, I picked up the large circle at one end and lifted—it was a very delicate, very finely linked leash, the clasp attached to a matching very delicate, very finely linked collar. I smiled to myself. Whoever put this gift together certainly spent a lot of money, I'd never seen a chain so expensively made, and whoever put this gift together definitely knew how to pick things out. That outfit had fit me perfectly, and my flesh already tingled at the feeling of cold metal against it.

Suddenly remembering a small makeup mirror in my bag, I fastened the collar around my neck, letting the leash hang down over my shirt. I couldn't resist. I opened up my mirror and looked at myself. I looked naughty. I couldn't remember the last time I felt naughty, much less looked naughty—and it felt good. I loved the way the chain looked against the collar of my white shirt, the metallic glitter of the leash against the sober gray of my suit. I ran my fingers down the metal and felt chills down my spine. Delicious.

I unclasped the leash from the collar and slid it into my bag. I kept the collar on. I wanted its cold reminder to stay with me for the rest of the afternoon. Doing my best to keep a straight face, I made my way back to my desk. I felt like everyone must have heard my moans or at least noticed the excessive time I had spent in the bathroom, but no one paid me any attention, no one commented on my pinkish cheeks or my unruly hair. I patted my hair anxiously as I sat back down at my computer, realizing I had forgotten to check my appearance in the mirror.

"Um, excuse me?"

The meek voice came from behind me, and I spun around guiltily. The girl had long curly brown hair and huge brown eyes behind small tortoiseshell frames. I noticed her lips, which were large and seemed just slightly dry and cracked. For an instant, I wondered what it would taste like to lick them wet.

"I really hate to bother you, but—"

"It's no problem," I said reassuringly. "What can I do for you?" She looked vaguely familiar, but I couldn't think from where. I tried to remember if I owed her any paperwork.

"This is terribly awkward," she flashed a nervous grin, her hands anxiously twisting together, "but, you see," and it all came out in one sudden rush. "I went out at lunch and I bought myself a present and I left it on my desk while I ran to answer the phone and the lunch receptionist thought it was for you because my name is also Rachel and the regular receptionist told her it was Rachel's box, and I don't know exactly how it happened but she told Michael and somehow he thought it was yours and I asked him if he'd seen it and he said oh no, he had thought it was for you, and he gave it to you, and I don't know if this makes any sense, but I wondered if you knew where my box was?"

I smiled. Of course. Of course it wasn't for me. Of course not. How ludicrous. Only in my life. I smiled at her, at this darling girl with the dry lips and the nervous hands.

"Nice to meet you, Rachel."

She laughed shyly, her hands resting for an instant against the edge of my desk.

"Why don't you have a seat?" I asked, motioning to my extra

chair. She sat down and stared at me, clearly wondering what I was going to say next.

"The box is here"—I gestured under my desk, showing her where I had tucked the package before my trip to the bathroom—"but the contents are in my bag. I'm sorry."

She looked at me, confused.

"I couldn't resist. I had to try it on."

She laughed again, a bit longer this time and a bit less shy.

I reached into my bag and pulled out Rachel's outfit and slipped it back into the box. The leash I placed carefully on top, before handing it all to her.

"I'm really sorry about this. You must think I am terribly strange." Her eyes stared straight into mine, wondering what I thought of her.

I smiled back at her. "Not at all. I think you are wonderful. It is the best birthday present I have ever gotten."

"It's your birthday today?" she exclaimed in wonder.

"Yes, yes, it is." I couldn't help smiling at this delightful girl.

"Oh God, I had no idea. Why, then you must keep this. It should be yours." She pushed the box back at me.

"No, no, no. It is yours. I got to try it on. That was amazing enough for me. It's your outfit. It belongs to you."

There was a pause while we both thought about what to say next.

"Please. I'd like you to have it."

I couldn't stop staring at her lips. "No, no, that's okay, it's not really me, anyway. I like my underwear to be brighter than the clothes I wear on top . . ."

She laughed again, this time the shyness almost gone, the brown eyes seemingly bigger and browner than before, and I began to notice little hints of gold inside them.

"You know," she leaned over to me and said, in a soft whisper, "they have corsets in red and pink and blue . . ."

My first thought was that her lips were only inches from mine. My second thought was that I'd never kissed a girl. My third thought was that a pink corset might be the best thing I could ever buy.

"Will you take me to the shop? I want to go."

"Of course!" she exclaimed. "If you won't let me give you mine as a birthday present, perhaps you can let me buy you another?"

"Only if you let me buy you a drink after?"

I couldn't believe it. I was flirting with a girl. I was flirting with a girl named Rachel. I was sitting at my desk, flirting with a girl with my name, and all I could think about was how her lips would feel between my teeth.

"I would love it," she said as she stood up. "Shall I stop by your desk at six?"

"That sounds great." I couldn't stop smiling at this creature.

She leaned over again, her lips inches from my face, and my breath stopped. What was she doing? Was she going to press her lips against mine, her tongue in my mouth, running against my teeth, her breath mixing with mine? Was she going to kiss me at my desk?

"You can keep the collar," she whispered, and she turned to walk away.

I closed my eyes, waiting for my heart to return to normal. Two more hours until six.

Alicia

"I want to learn how to make you come," she whispered in my ear.

I could feel her breath hot on the back of my neck, her hand snaking its way around my waist, her hips pressed behind me, but the only thing that registered were those words, those words and the space between us. Her breath continued, slow and steady, while I stood there, making my palms and my neck sweat, and she waited for my response.

I didn't know what to say. I knew who this girl was, even though I hadn't seen her face all night. I closed my eyes and let mind refresh memory. I closed my eyes, held on to the bar with my hands, and let Alicia fill the space behind my eyelids. I couldn't resist smiling while

I pictured her, knowing that, when I turned around, it would be her mouth inches from mine.

Her breath continued on my neck as she waited, knowing that she had me and, with that fact solidly assured, she had all the time in the world. I gave it another fifteen seconds, indulging myself in the mental picture I'd drawn, then I turned around to see the real thing.

God, Alicia was the hottest girl I'd ever seen. She stood at least six feet, her black hair cropped short and boyish, her hips hung low, and her arms lean and well-defined. She'd been a track star in college and never lost her runner's body. Her eyes, which stared straight into mine so unflinchingly that I had to look down, were the kind of blue that makes you realize how often you are disappointed in the sky.

It was impossible to look at her lips without thinking of eating them.

The thing that got me most of all about Alicia, the thing that made me get wet and quivery even when I saw her from a block away, was her wallet chain. A million punk rockers wear them and look ridiculous, but, on her, the silver strand that ran from hip to ass was hypnotic and sexy and made me want to fuck her like nothing else. There was something about the way it hung, gently cresting off her waist, swinging ever so slightly as she moved, the little loops glittering in the stray light, that made me want to grab it, to yank it, to pull it out of her pocket, wrenching her to me.

But until tonight, I'd only stared at the chain, fantasizing about it. There had been one lucky night a week or two earlier, when she had stood in front of me at the bar, and I delicately ran my finger over it while she ordered her drink. She didn't notice, of course, and I didn't say a word. How could I? It was Alicia, after all.

I figured that would be the closest I'd come to her and her chain and those perfect hips, but then tonight—tonight her breath had been on my neck, her words still lingering in the air between us. I just looked at her while she looked steadily back at me. We held it like that for what felt like an hour—an hour when the bar grew silent and everyone else vanished. My world existed merely to hold her across from me, until she smiled—the grin racing to split her face, lips revealing small white teeth—and then life hit Play again. The music surged back into my ears, and I almost flinched from the shock.

"Hey," she said, tilting her head like John Wayne, "did I scare you?"

"Oh God no," I rushed to respond, my mind frantic to get the words out quickly enough to allay her fears but still slowly enough to make my reassurance appear convincing. "Not at all. I mean—"

"Prove it."

I looked at her, too stunned for an instant to say anything, before figuring what the fuck. I dove right in. I grabbed the chain with my right hand, her waist with my left, and pulled her to me. I don't remember which hit first—her lips or her hips—but before I knew it, both of them were pressed up against me, my tongue tasting hers for the first time.

She tasted like whiskey and cigarettes, like motorcycles with a hint of lip gloss. I held her to me, afraid that the second she pulled back for air she'd realize she was kissing the wrong girl. I kept our lips locked, running my tongue against her teeth, hoping I'd keep her distracted until—until what? I don't know, I guess until either I'd had enough (which would never happen) or until she'd been kissed long enough to fall under my spell.

Not quite believing my luck, I savored her taste while my hands ran over her hips, the hips that I'd stared at from across streets and across rooms—so slim and yet so low. She had the Western stance with the boyish figure that killed me every time, and I couldn't get enough. I felt the ridges of her pants, the seams on her pockets, the chill of her chain, the rough fabric of her jeans, and the smooth hint of her underwear along her waist. I felt it all—quickly, rapidly—eager to consume her before she could disappear.

I had no idea why Alicia had decided to kiss me that night, but I wasn't going to ask any questions. I wasn't going to say anything, in fact, because I wouldn't give her the opportunity to reconsider. I wouldn't stop kissing her until she made me. I kept my tongue in her mouth, my hands on her waist, my fingers wrapped around her chain, desperate to absorb it all.

I felt myself falling into a daze, the voices around me disappearing, the world becoming full of only her and the rhythmic bass beats from the dj's records. My eyes closed, all I saw was black—and all I felt was her. I couldn't think of anything more perfect, until she pulled her head back to look me in the eyes, and the ground opened up beneath me. I could barely look back.

"Hey."

I smiled at her nervously. "Hey."

"I meant it," she said.

"What's that?"

She stared at me for an instant before leaning over to place her lips against my ear. "I want to make you come." There was a pause while I felt her hot breath on my face, and I wondered if I'd be able to keep standing. "Will you teach me how?"

I leaned forward just enough to bring my lips to her ear. "Where should we go?"

Alicia pulled her head back and gave me a steady look. "I figured we could get started here," she said, as her hand slid up my skirt, pushing aside my underwear.

I had to grab the stool beside me for support. I couldn't breathe. All I felt were her cool fingers pressing against my wet thighs as she kept staring straight into my eyes.

"Do you, I mean, I don't kn—"

"Shh," she said, leaning over, her lips mere inches from my face. "Don't worry—no one's watching."

I looked around, barely able to move my head while every part of my body was focused directly between my legs. In the slow motion of my gaze, it appeared to be true—no one was watching. We were in the corner of the room, my back to the wall. Alicia was facing me, so whatever she was doing to me was blocked from view by her body. The room was dark, and most of the other girls seemed more concerned with finishing their drinks and finding dates than what we were doing, but still—my brain couldn't quite process what was happening.

Just when I started to come to terms with the fact that this gorgeously sexy girl had slipped her fingers up my skirt and into my underwear, my lungs froze, my heart stopped beating, and the world came to a sudden halt as she suddenly shoved her fingers inside my pussy, up through the warm, wet space and against the front wall, sending waves of electric pleasure into my entire body.

I felt the very unglamorous feeling of my eyes rolling back in my head. I slumped against the back of my stool, my hands hanging weakly at my sides, control of my body having been handed over to the six-foot figure who was still staring intently at me. No one had ever made me feel like this before, and I didn't think it was simply because no one's fingers had ever been this long.

I couldn't move, I couldn't do anything but sit there and let her press inside me again and again and again, each time my body reeling with pleasure and pure sensation, each time my pussy filling up with wetness, my clitoris swelling.

With every touch, the feeling heightened, and I became less able to respond like a functioning adult. I was convinced that everyone in the bar must be staring at me in this ridiculous position. I tried to get Alicia to stop just long enough so that I could collect my senses, so that I could look around and make sure people weren't pointing, so that I could figure out what, exactly, was going on. I tried to push her hand away, but she just leaned over, closer, and whispered in my ear.

"I'm not going to stop. I'm not going to stop until you tell me something else to do."

I couldn't get the words out. I knew I should have had something to say, but I couldn't say it. At first, I couldn't because my brain couldn't form the words, and then I couldn't because Alicia had started licking my lips. I didn't know which sensation was more acute—her tongue, gently flicking at the outer edges of my mouth, or her fingers, which were still pressed far inside me. I felt like I had become a vessel for pure sensation, and there was no room left for anything else.

My entire body tried to curve around her fingers. I didn't care anymore that people were talking and smoking and drinking all around us. I couldn't quite forget that they were there, but I couldn't see straight enough to see them. I sort of heard them, but they were drowned out by the buzzing in my ears, my hearing apparently sacrificed as the other senses took over. I smelled Alicia, her scent wafting toward me with every move she made, filling my nostrils and lungs as her fingers filled the cavity between my legs. She smelled like hair products and perfume, beer and cigarettes, leather and sweat. Just like she seemed larger than life, her scent seemed to consume anything else that might have been in the air. I took in huge gulps of it—that is, when I was remembering to breathe.

When I wasn't remembering to breathe, my body was bent around her fingers, pushing her in, deeper and harder, making her fingers slide into the space they were made to fit. Just when I thought I couldn't feel anything more, when the pleasure couldn't possibly get any more intense, Alicia did an extraordinary thing that I can only attribute, again, to the length of her fingers, or perhaps her remarkable dexterity. While keeping two of her fingers pressed solidly against my G-spot, still maintaining pressure and movement, she placed her thumb on my clitoris and began to rub in small, methodical circles.

If it hadn't felt so incredible, I might have passed out.

I slumped farther back in the stool, my face set in an expression of complete ecstasy. By this point, I was sure I was making a spectacle of myself, but what could I do? There was no way in hell I'd let Alicia stop; all I wanted was more, more, more. I didn't think I'd be able to breathe again until she'd finished coaxing me slowly and skillfully to orgasm. So I lay back, just barely aware of the people and the noise surrounding us, wondering how she managed to fit her fingers so far inside without letting up pressure on my clitoris.

I could feel the pleasure coming in waves, rolling up from between my legs, making my stomach tense up and my lungs contract. Her fingers would press against my G-spot and slide out, tantalizing me as they grazed the opening, then slipping their way back in to repeat the pressure. In and out, slowly building up speed and momentum, all the while never letting up her methodical, rhythmic pressure on my clitoris.

"Do you like it?" she asked, breathing into my ear.

I envied her that ability to breathe, that ability to inhale and exhale. I felt like steel girders had replaced my lungs as I clenched the sides of the stool in an effort to utter some kind of response.

"Well?" she asked again, that grin back on her face as her fingers slid back out of my pussy and ran down my thigh, leaving wet trails behind them.

"Oh God, don't stop," I said, before I could think of anything else to say, before I had a second to realize how weak desperation always sounds.

"What's that?" She smiled at me, her fingers now making wet circles on my knee.

"I asked you not to stop." I tried to make my reply sound cool and easy, not as if I was actually making a fool of myself in the middle of a crowded bar, my voice a pathetic plea, my entire self bent backward on the chair to facilitate whatever angle she selected.

"So you liked it then?"

"Yes. Yes, yes, yes."

She leaned over close, putting her lips directly outside my ear. "Anything else you want me to do?"

I didn't answer.

Alicia stood back and gave me a long stare before leaning back over to continue, "I really want to see you come."

The world swirled around me. I tried to breathe.

"Will you tell me how I can do that?"

How she could do that? My entire insides were aching. My entire body was a tightly wound knot of sexual frustration. I was convinced that there must be a puddle between my legs. My underwear was drenched, my clitoris screaming for attention. I felt hyperawake, so desperate for release, that she could have touched me, and I would have melted on the floor in a mess of sighs and moans.

She stood in front of me, and I felt like looking at her might be pleasure enough—it would have been pleasure enough if I could only forget how amazing her fingers had felt, or how intensely I wanted them back. Just looking at her right hand, as it rested on my knee, made it impossible for me to think of anything but those five fingers and what they could do.

"I want you back inside me," I told her. "You're killing me. I want more. I want your fingers back where they were, and I want to feel my fingers inside you."

She gave me a huge grin.

"That sounds perfect. Come."

She grabbed my hand in hers and pulled me behind her. I grabbed my coat and hurried after her. We went to the back of the bar and turned to go down the stairs.

"What's down there?"

"Don't worry," she replied, over her shoulder, as we made our way into the darkness, "it's the storage room. I've got a key."

I followed her into the dimly lit room, past some empty liquor boxes, behind a couple shelves of beer bottles, to a red vinyl couch littered with some paper and stray cups. She brushed the debris off and pushed me down on the couch. Standing over me, she reached under my skirt and pulled off my underwear, never letting her eyes leave mine.

She glanced briefly at my underwear before tossing them to the side. I saw her smile to herself when she noticed how wet they were. Then, pushing my legs apart, she turned her attention back to me. She ran her hands down my thighs, right hand on left leg, left hand on right leg, running them over the curve of my thigh, circling my knee, going down to the edge of my boots. She lingered there for a second before bringing her fingers slowly back up my leg, stopping on my knees for what felt like an eternity, while I spread my legs as far apart as I possibly could. Oh God, I wanted her fingers inside me—just seeing them on my legs, noticing their delicate length and perfect shape, made my insides ache.

Her ripe red fingernails stood out in the dark room, looking almost black against my white skin. Still looking straight at me, Alicia squeezed my knees and, with a small sigh, knelt between my legs. I couldn't believe it. Her body was now officially between my legs, her hands making their slow way up my thighs. I could feel her hot breath on my skin while her face came closer to me.

Her fingers pressed into my thighs, inches away from my clitoris, which was aching to be touched, and my pussy, which was aching to be filled. As if she were completely unaware of how desperately I wanted her to cross those few inches, she grabbed my thighs and stared at me. Her nails dug into my skin, the little red orbs making perfect circles on top of my flesh. I moaned, a combination of frustration and complete desire. Her fingers deep against my thighs, she pulled them back, pulling my pussy lips apart in the process. I inhaled sharply, feeling the cold air rushing inside me, in marked contrast to the hot wetness between my legs.

Grinning at me, she leaned over and flicked my clit with the tip of tongue. Feeling as though I might drown in red naugahyde, she skirted over the outside of my pussy with her tongue, using just enough pressure to make my skin feel like it was on fire. I arched my hips at her, craving a slip of her tongue, her fingers, something inside me, but she shook her head and pulled back.

With perfect precision, with impeccable slowness and care, Alicia took her first two fingers and slipped them into her mouth. The sight of those fingers disappearing between those red lips nearly killed me. I watched the red nails slide in and out the matching lips—red on red on white. The part of my brain that could still think appreciated the aesthetic perfection of the moment—but most of my brain had rushed between my legs and was an aching disaster.

I'd stopped wondering why Alicia was doing this and just wanted her to take it all the way.

She pulled two very wet fingers out of her mouth and pressed them flatly against my spread pussy lips, her wet fingers making flat circles around my lips. She started to push in as though she wanted to put her fingers in me the long way, her fingers parallel to my lips, the tips at my clit, palm cupping my ass while I slipped even farther forward on the couch.

"How does it feel?"

I was so dazed and dizzy, I didn't even realize that she was speaking. Her fingers slid out, bringing me to attention by the loss of her inside me. I looked down for a second, but, before I could see anything, she replaced her fingers. Assuming that my silence meant I needed more, this time it was three. She let some spit leak down from her mouth and onto her hand. It was starting to get sloppy—my juices mixing with hers—and I knew I was leaking everywhere. I could hear wet sounds coming from between my legs.

The tightness I felt when she introduced her third finger had changed to a satisfying fullness, and I arched against her, trying to push her deeper inside. I could feel myself relaxing inside to accommodate her, while her pinky tapped against the lower part of my pussy, occasionally brushing against my ass. She must have been able to tell what she was doing to me, since each time she licked at my clit, more of my fluid leaked down my crotch. I could feel a small pool of moisture building up under me and wondered, briefly, if it was possible to stain naugahyde.

Her fingers came out again, and I was freshly distracted by the thrill of feeling her slipping them back in. They felt amazing. I'd never felt anything this far inside me, never felt so full and alive and electric, as though every skin cell on my inner walls had just been awakened. The combination of fingers inside and fingers outside sent a dizzying overload of sensation to my brain. It was almost too much to have it both ways, but, at the same time, all I wanted was more.

As if sensing my overload, and loving the power it gave her, she took her left hand and, while keeping her right hand inside me, pushed my tank top up to my shoulders, pulling my bra down, underneath my breasts. Leaning over, she ran her tongue up my stomach, to the center of my chest, then in looping circles around my nipples. Totally teasing me, she flicked her tongue over their surface momentarily before pulling back to run her mouth back over my neck, chest, and waist.

Gradually, she brought her tongue closer to my nipples, running back and forth over them, her spit sending liquid streaks down my chest. While her tongue licked, her perfect white teeth closed over the tips of my nipples, not biting so much as just pressing down around them. The combination of the pain and the pleasure made me dizzy. I tried to put my arms around her, to pull her close, but between her movements between my legs and her movements across my breasts, my arms were useless.

Just as the sensation became too acute, she slipped her hand out and spread her two fingers into a Y shape before leaning over to lick the exposed part of my pussy. It felt like she had just spread the most exquisite trail of fire, leaving me quivering in her wake. Pleased with my response, she continued to run her tongue from bottom to top over and over again, each time leaving me more of a wreck than the time before, as every part of my body appeared to rush between my legs.

Gradually increasing her pressure, she never let up her perfect rhythm. Each time, she would start at the bottom, at the base of my opening, and then she would slowly run her tongue over the opening, letting it linger just enough to gently caress the surface inside, before making her way up to my clit, where she would press just a bit harder, make two or three of the tiniest of circles, then slip her way down to start over.

I was barely aware that my nails were digging into the naugahyde on either side of my legs.

As she coaxed me to totally inexperienced heights of agony and frustration, a victim of her slow and methodical technique, she sent me reeling by slipping her fingers back inside me— never once letting up on the rhythm of her tongue. With that combination, it was over in less than a minute. Between the internal pressure and the external pressure and the smooth softness of her tongue and the persistent pushing of her fingers, the stimulation on the clitoris and inside my pussy, on my G-spot and everywhere, I crumbled.

With a huge moan, the tingle started at my toes and rapidly consumed my body. Something unintelligible came out of my lips as my body fell limply against the couch, and Alicia, with one parting lick, slowly drew her fingers out from inside me.

I just looked at her in awe. I still had no idea who this beautiful creature was, or why she had chosen me, but I wasn't going to ask any questions. I couldn't even talk, for starters, and, in my daze, I was even more transfixed by her beauty than before. She looked at me for a moment, then stood up. Leaning over, she gave me a delicious, lingering kiss, full of my taste and hers and the intensity of what had just happened. I tried to mutter something about how it was her turn, but she shook her head and gave me one more kiss.

"I'm more than satisfied," she said. "I've been wanting to do that to you for a long time."

With that, she gave me one more kiss and helped me stand up.

"Leave your underwear down here. It'll make it easier for me to touch you later tonight."

I stared at her as I followed her back up the stairs. Watching her hips move in front of me, the silver chain swinging just so, I couldn't believe what had happened, I couldn't believe that I remembered how that chain had felt in my hand, or that we were going back upstairs to do it all over again.

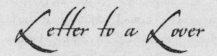

Letter to a Lover

I wish you were going to be at home tonight. I wish you were going to be there when I opened the door. I wish I could open the door and find your naked body standing in the hallway.

I'd drop my bag, drop my coat, drop it all on the floor, and I'd head straight for you, grabbing you around the waist and throwing you against the wall. I'd dig my fingers into your skin, my tongue in your mouth, your cock already hard between my legs.

I'd ravage you.

I want to feel you underneath me. I want you on my bed. I'd push you there, push you down, push you where I wanted you, then I'd stand over you and look down at you. I'd look at you like you were mine—which you are, but I mean all mine. As though I truly possessed you. Which, of course, in that moment, I would.

I would look down at you, at the fine gold hairs on your chest, at the lean muscular arms I would kick to the head of the bed, at your perfectly lean waist, neatly framed between my feet, at the bike-messenger thighs—I'd look at it all, your green eyes staring back at me, your short blond hair, your long fingers that I can't look at without craving them inside me. I'd look at you, standing above you, until I couldn't stand it anymore. Then I'd fall down, laughing, knees on either side of your chest, and I'd kiss, kiss, kiss you. I'd kiss you all over. I'd run my fingers down your arms and my tongue over your chest, kisses on your mouth, your cheeks, your shoulders, your neck.

(Oh God, I'm already twitching in my seat just thinking about it.)

I'm looking at you. I'm totally naked, you're totally naked, and I possess you. I've kicked your arms above your head, my feet are pressed on either side of your waist—you can't move. I've got you. All you can do is look at me as I look at you. Then I slip down, knees on either side of your chest, my pussy on your stomach. You can feel the damp heat leaking onto your skin. Your cock is hard between my legs, pressed up against my ass.

I take my finger and slip it into your mouth. I tell you to lick it as I run it around the edges of your lips and across your tongue. While you're licking, I gently slide back, lifting up my ass as I go, so that your cock slips in right between my legs, filling my pussy as though our two parts had been built to fit each other. I take my finger out of your mouth, and I make you talk dirty to me. I make you tell me how hot I make you, how much I turn you on, how you want to ram yourself inside of me until I almost split in two. I make you tell me how much you love my breasts, my hips, my waist and thighs, how much I drive you mad with desire, how you can't think of anything but fucking me, how swollen and frustrated you are. I make you tell me how much you want it, how hard you want to fuck me, while all I do is sit on your cock, but I don't move—I just feel you hard and solid inside me.

Then I kneel on the floor in front of you leaving you on the bed, looking over at my ass as I spread my legs. You run your hand down my stomach, feeling the hair on my pussy. Your fingers dip inside my open cunt—it's wet, creamy, dirty. You want to see it and taste it. You get up to move behind me, putting your hand on my back and pushing me forward. My ass is spread wide and in the air, my pussy lips parted and glistening. You draw your face close to smell me, putting your nose to my lips, moving up to my ass. You can't get enough.

Sliding the tip of your tongue between my parted lips, you lightly lick my clit, and then press your head deep into me—in and out, in and out. You taste enough to make you want to taste more, more, more. Your tongue heads over to my asshole, makes a small circle, then back into my pussy again. Wrapping your lips around mine, your tongue slips across my clit. Your cock is so hard—I can see it when I look between my legs. It's sticking straight out, the veins prominent, the skin glistening, and all I want is to feel it fill me up, but I don't do anything, I just wait and savor the desire. I wait to see what you do next.

My pussy is so wet from your mouth and my juices that you can't help wiping your hand against it. You can't stop staring at it, desiring it, wanting to touch it and taste it and push yourself inside it. You take your wet hand to your cock, stroking it while you eat my pussy with slow, deep licks of your tongue. I shove myself against your face, wanting your tongue and your fingers inside me, my emptiness suddenly large and looming and unbearable. I can't imagine not having you inside me, a part of me is missing without you, and I grow wetter and more restless with every passing second; with every passing lick of your tongue all I can think about is that I want more, more, more.

You stand up and look down at my wet crotch—your cock is shining, the tip of your head pushing slightly against my lips. I want it so badly. I am aching for you.

I tilt my ass and my hips toward you, pushing back, trying to get you inside me, but you slip back just enough so that all I get is a passing touch. You grab hold of your cock and start massaging me with it, from the base of my clit upward, echoing your tongue's earlier movements. I can't stand it—I start to moan, desperately shoving myself against you. You slip your head inside me, just a little, just enough to tease me. I feel tight. You love it.

You pull out and continue to massage me with it, leaning forward to feel my breasts. You cup one with your hand, my hard nipple against your palm, your face against my back, your cock against my ass. You smell the musky scent of my armpit, and it turns you on as you pinch my nipple—both of us getting harder by the second.

Your hand makes its way up my neck while you squeeze me lightly. You move back, and your cock finally enters my tight pussy. As the head goes in, the foreskin gets pushed back by the walls of my cunt. You feel the tough ridges inside me. You go all the way in, and I sigh with delicious relief, every inch of my skin grateful and electrified. Then you pull out—my white creamy juices covering your cock. You take a second to rub the juices, to feel their wetness all over your skin, before pushing your way back in. Each time you pull out and go back, I am wetter than the last, and you love it. The wetter I am, the harder you get. You hold a handful of my hair in your fist while the other hand still firmly grips my breast, as you pick up speed.

Soon your cock is slamming inside of me—very hard, very rough—and I keep shoving myself against you, matching your rhythm and intensity. You pull out again, and a droplet of cum drips out of your cock, between my legs, onto my clit, and my fingers are there to receive it. I almost can't tell which wetness is yours and which is mine.

(I have so much sexual frustration that it runs in my veins instead of blood. I feel like I've forgotten what it's like to have someone explore my body even though it's only been six hours since you left my bed.)

But I know which wetness is yours, because it's white and the texture is different, and I slip my finger into my mouth and taste you, and it just makes me want to taste more. I'm tired of being on the bottom, so I turn myself over, shoving you off me and onto the bed. It's my turn now. I don't want to be teased anymore. I can't wait. I want what I want, and I want you inside me—but I want to start with you inside my mouth.

I slide my way down your body and wrap my mouth around your beautifully hard cock.

(Oh God, I want you, I want you, I want you.)

Ever so slowly at first, I start by running my tongue along the edges of your cock, along the tip and the shaft and the base and the balls and the skin, licking you like you were the most delicious ice-cream sundae, and I can't get enough of the sugar and the cold and the chocolate and the cherries and the syrup, and my tongue goes everywhere and I lick and kiss and just heave deep hot breaths of desire and all you can do is squirm and beg for more.

I lick until I've tasted it all, then I just put you all into my mouth. I let you fill me up, let your cock slide into the space between my cheek and my jaw, let it go so far down my throat it meets the back of it. I pull back and come in, I run you along my teeth, along my lips, along my tongue, inside and outside, into my cheek and delicately between the teeth. You can't stop moaning, and I am eating you up as though I'd never had anything this good in my life. You are perfect. You fit perfectly inside me.

I start moving my head in tempo—letting you slide out and then into my cheek, out and down my throat, letting you come all the way in, then pausing just long enough for my tongue to run down the length of you, and I let you slip out as my teeth run along the edge of your shaft, sending electric waves down your spine and up my arms. I'm moving rapidly now, concentrating on maintaining perfect pressure and perfect speed. You are completely at my mercy, begging me not to stop, telling me how good it feels, and please-please-please don't stop.

I don't stop. I keep going. This is what I want. I want to feel you inside me, feeling you get harder and longer because of my teeth and tongue and lips and mouth.

I slip my right hand around the base of your cock and start to move it back and forth, in tandem with my mouth. My hand allows my mouth to stay closer to your head, focusing on licking you, letting my mouth move back and forth along the ridge of your head, while my hand starts moving rapidly at your shaft—quick, quick, quick.

You're on the verge of complete release, of letting go, and I stop.

I've made you hot and wet and completely beside yourself with desire, and the timing is perfect—it's time for you to push your way inside me. Your cock slides into me, slippery with the wetness of my juices and yours. You are beside yourself, you are so close to coming. I am beside myself because my body has been aching for this—feeling you in my mouth has made me as hot as if you were between my legs, only without the sensation of satisfaction I have now.

(I am shifting back and forth in my seat as I write this, staring restlessly out the window, wishing the world would stop so that I could run and find you and wrap myself around your perfect body. I can't stand being here, feeling so far away from you, the only consolation the smell of you still on my fingers and the fantasies of what I will do to you when I see you next.)

I start riding you, faster and faster, shoving you inside me, deeper and harder, arching my back and shoving my hips forward so that your cock pushes against my front wall, pressing against my G-spot and sending waves of pleasure between my legs and up my back. The quicker I go, the more the waves accelerate, until I can barely breathe, and you can barely breathe, and we are both picking up speed, you with your hands on my waist, lifting me up and pulling me down, as we maintain our increasing tempo. I shove against you, my clitoris full and aching and my G-spot about to release, your cock in as far as it can go, but it's still not far enough, and we keep pushing against each other, trying to get you farther inside.

You tell me, barely able to get the words out, that you're about to come and I tell you to let go—I can't stand a second more, as my walls collapse, and my blood rushes to my head, the sensation filling me with electricity, and you pulse even faster before heaving a huge sigh, and the world stops, time stops, nothing moves, there is no sound, no action, just a huge pause in the face of it all, and we collapse, consumed with our pleasure.

I fall down on top of you, my sweat mingling with your sweat, my body damp against yours, and I just lie on your chest and feel your breathing, letting you lift me with every inhale.

(I can't take it anymore. I can't sit still. I've got to have you now. I'm going home to wait for you there. Whenever you come, I'll be ready.)

Alex

Her fingers traced the line of my cheekbone, but I still couldn't bring myself to look her in the eye.

"Are you okay?" she asked softly.

I just nodded, looking away.

"Will. Over here."

Gently grabbing my chin with her hand, she turned my head toward her.

"What's going on?"

"Nothing. Nothing, I swear." My palms were sweating. I desperately wanted to wipe them on my jeans, but I didn't want to move, I didn't want to do anything that might give her a clue what was going through my head. I just stayed frozen, willing the perspiration to stop, willing my body to cool down. Cool down, cool down, cool it.

"Will, what's going on? Please talk to me."

Her eyes kept trying to find mine as mine stayed firmly fixed on the floor, until she leaned over to run her lips over mine. Her lips felt like silk. She pressed harder, tongue pushing its way into my mouth. I could feel her warmth, her softness, and my stomach froze. I lost sight of anything else. She kissed me harder as I couldn't help responding, my tongue in her mouth, our teeth and lips pushing against each other. Her arm slid around my waist, her hand under my shirt, my heart racing—until I remembered everything and pulled away.

"I'm sorry, I can't. I can't. I'm sorry."

I got up off the bed and started to move toward the door.

"Come back here!" She grabbed my shirt with her hand, pulling me back onto the bed. I fell against her, and she laughed as she wrapped her arms around me.

"You can't just leave like that! Please. Talk to me, Will."

I felt her arms tightly locked around my chest, her long thin legs entwined around mine, her body holding me as hard as she could. I lay there, her breasts against my back, her hips against my ass, every inch of her lean body against every corresponding inch of mine. I could feel my lust for her rushing through me. I could feel myself desperate with desire for her, and I knew that she knew how much I wanted her.

People always stared at her—even when she was offstage. People looked at her in the supermarket, in the park, on the street. Even in sweatpants, she had something. It wasn't just her green eyes or her blond hair—she had something that took over a room, something you didn't even realize was there until it was gone, then you wondered why everything had suddenly turned quiet and dark and become a lot less interesting. You didn't realize, until she left the room, that it was her electricity making things move, and, that, when she left, everyone and everything got a little flat.

But when she was onstage? Jesus Christ. The first time I saw her band, I forgot about everything else—why I was there, who I was, anything that had mattered before just disappeared, replaced by this image of something I couldn't explain, couldn't categorize, couldn't dismiss.

I'd never seen anyone like her—white-blond hair sticking up all over the place, green eyes ringed in layers of the blackest eyeliner, legs that went on forever with these black thigh-high stockings ringed in pink lace, and a T-shirt missing more parts than it had left. All torn and ripped and safety-pinned, everything blending into this mix of color and metal, but I still couldn't take my eyes off her face. It glowed in the middle of everything else, the stage lighting unnecessary. And her eyes? Those green eyes? I knew I'd never find my way back out of them.

I vaguely noticed the other members of her band, but the only time I took my eyes off her face was when she looked at me—and then I had to look anywhere but at her. I couldn't bear to look her straight in the eyes. When her eyes looked into mine, my body froze, my heart and lungs and stomach in a seizure of time. I had to stare at the floor, her voice filling my ears, while I watched the floorboards and didn't see a thing.

When she wasn't looking at me, though, that's when I was looking at her—at the way her arms moved, the way she stood, the way she laughed, the way she sang, the way she thrust herself at the audience, the way she held their attention in the palm of her hand, coaxing them closer, farther, higher. I watched her tease them—and pretended she was only teasing me.

She must have been able to tell that I was watching her, because she kept looking at me, and I had to keep looking at the floor, at her guitarist, at her drummer, at the mike stand—anything that didn't have those green eyes. Anything that didn't carry her kind of voltage.

Halfway through the set, she pulled a T-shirt out of a bag at her feet and threw it at me. I watched it hit me square in the chest before looking up—right at her. Everything lurched like a roller coaster, and I ached for something more substantial than a cotton-poly blend to hold on to.

She grinned at me. I blushed and looked away, clenching the shirt in my hand. What the hell was I supposed to do? Oh God, what was I supposed to do?

And then, without warning, the set was over, leaving me to twist the shirt in my hands, wondering if I could just turn around and walk away, if I would ever manage to feel the same way again, if I could really just leave, but if I didn't leave what could I possibly say, and—

"Hi."

I looked up. Standing less than a foot away from me. All I could do was swallow and stare.

"Aren't you Pete's brother?"

I nodded. Speech eluded me.

She smiled broadly, and I thought I might have lost my stomach to my feet.

"That's what I thought. Thanks for coming tonight. Do you want to sign our mailing list?" She thrust a pad of paper at me with a pen.

I took both and wrote out my e-mail address as slowly as I could, trying to figure out what I could say to make her stay and talk to me. Come on, Will, don't be a total prick. Pull something together. She's here, talking to you. Say something, you idiot—but words failed me.

"Nice to meet you properly," she said, offering me her hand and giving me a smile. "You're better-looking than Peter, you know?"

Then she tapped me on the shoulder with her pad of paper and spun around to continue her mailing list duties, leaving me to stand there, letting it all sink in.

Was she just being nice? She wasn't flirting, was she? I mean, she wouldn't really think I looked like Peter, would she? Was I supposed to flirt back? I didn't know how to flirt with her,

I didn't know what to say, so I just held her band's T-shirt in my hand, trying to think of all the ways I could fuck up this moment, trying desperately to think of the one way that maybe I wouldn't.

I watched her move around the room, the mess of blond hair and long legs and white skirt and whiter teeth, and I knew I didn't stand a chance. Who was I kidding? What the hell was I thinking? Fuck it. People like me never get people like her. I left.

I don't know what came first, the voice in my ear or the hand on my arm.

"Were you just going to leave without saying good-bye?"

"I'm sorry, you looked busy, I figured I would just head out, and, uh—"

I hadn't thought it was possible to feel like more of an idiot than before—but now I did.

"Want to buy me a drink?"

Her face glistened a bit with sweat, her hair in little spikes around her head—and I couldn't take my eyes off her glistening mouth long enough to notice anything else.

"I'd love to."

"Great," she said, beaming. Grabbing my hand, she pulled me after her to the bar. "I've actually got a stack of drink tickets, so I can get you whatever you want—on me."

Even though I wouldn't have thought it possible, after two hours and several drinks each, I was even more in love with her than before. I loved her blond hair, the brilliant green eyes ringed in smudged black liner, the mouth that never stopped talking, the lips that made me want to bite my own and pretend they were hers—and when I stopped staring at her face for a minute, I couldn't keep my eyes away from the line of her shoulders, the perfect way the bone ran just under her neck, the little beads of sweat that gathered in the small circle, and the small glimpses I could steal of the line leading down between her breasts.

It all looked so perfect, I had to keep gripping my glass so tightly I worried it would shatter—or I would have worried that it would shatter if I had any bit of mind left to think about things like breaking glass. Instead, I thought about her, her, her—and let her words fall like rationed drops into my ear, while I stared at her, trying as hard as I could to memorize every second because I was convinced this would never happen again.

Until—"Want to get out of here?"

I blinked. What?

"Come on"—she tugged at my sleeve—"we've been here long enough!"

"Um, sure, okay—but where do you want to go?" I don't know if I was more flustered by trying to get my coat off the stool or by what she had said.

She smiled. "Well, I've got to bring my gear home before we go anywhere else, so why don't you walk me home, then we can figure it out?"

She lived around the corner from the bar, so it didn't take long until I was sitting on her bed watching her race around her room, dropping her gear in specific corners ("God, this place is a mess"), stripping off some of her extra jewelry ("too many chains, eh?"), changing the music after every song ("dammit, I don't know what I want to listen to"), checking her appearance in the mirror ("I think I might need a shower, I'm covered in sweat")—but it didn't matter what she was doing, I couldn't concentrate on a single word.

I couldn't concentrate because I couldn't stop staring at the precious pale stretch of skin between the end of her skirt and the start of her stockings. I kept staring at the elastic of her garter belt, watching the way it pressed into her soft skin, the little indentations it made as she moved. I tried not to, but I couldn't stop imagining what was under the skirt, and what it would feel like to run my fingers across the lace, up over the skin, and then under the skirt. I tried not to, but I couldn't stop wondering what color her underwear was and what it would feel like to touch it.

It was pink. I knew because she finally sat down on the couch, across from me, and spread her legs. I saw the pink, I saw where the underwear met the garters, and then I quickly looked away, feeling my cheeks turn red while my hands started to sweat.

She didn't seem to notice, still talking about whatever it was she was talking about, while I stared at the wall and tried not to think of the soft warmth between her legs, the dark heat just three feet from me. Her legs stayed open, while she stayed completely oblivious to the effect she was having on me.

And then, suddenly, I realized she was talking about this dream she'd had the other night, about how she was dating this guy, and they'd gone to bed, but she wanted some water, so she went out to the kitchen to get some, with just a towel wrapped around herself, because it was late, and she didn't think anyone else would be up. Only thing was, when she walked through the living room, her boyfriend's younger brother was there, still up, working on his computer. The only light in the room was the blue glow of the monitor, but it was enough light for them to see each other, and it was enough light for her to notice that he was getting hard through his boxer shorts while she was talking to him. She laughed a bit, asking him if she turned him on. He got all embarrassed and blushed, and she said no, no, it's okay, don't be embarrassed, and then she leaned over and kissed him. Of course, the towel fell off, and then she was totally naked, kneeling on the carpet, while he was on the chair, and they kissed, and kissed, and she reached one hand down between his legs and started rubbing him, then she went down on him, and he came, and she kissed him once more, and she went to the kitchen, got her water, and went back to bed.

I am reeling. My dick is pressing against my pants, and I am staring at the wall as hard as I possibly can, thinking of anything I can to distract myself, and she is still sitting there, her legs spread just enough for me to see up her skirt, only now she isn't talking anymore—she is just looking at me, smiling.

"Why don't you come over here?" she asks me, patting the seat next to her.

I absolutely could not handle this. "I think I'd better go. It must be late." I start to get up.

"No, come on, not yet. Please? Just a little while longer?"

She pats the seat next to her again and smiles. I can't resist her. Why am I bothering to try? My stomach is churning, I know I should leave, but I can't. I sit down next to her.

"So are you still dating that girl?"

I say no before I think to ask how she knew whom I was dating, anyway.

"Oh, that's too bad," she says, and I am too busy trying to figure out how she knew about me and Sarah to notice that it seems like she doesn't mean it at all.

"How was she?"

"She was nice, but, uh, we didn't have much in common." I really don't know why she cares.

"No, I mean, how was she?"

She says it slowly, so slowly, that I don't know if I should pay attention to the feeling of her breath on my face, or to the slightly drunk, very sexy sound of her voice, or to her hand, which is only inches from my thigh.

I stop noticing all of that when she moves her legs, when she slowly shifts her right leg over her left leg, and I hear the smooth sound of skin against skin, and all I can think about is how much I want my hand in that space between right thigh and left thigh.

Then I realize she is looking me, watching me, waiting for me to answer her question. With tremendous force of effort, I pull my brain back from between her legs.

"She was okay, I guess."

"Hmm, boring, huh?"

"Yeah, sorta." I desperately want to leave. I desperately need to get myself out of there.

"I know what you need." And then she uncrosses her legs again, spreading her right leg until it touches my left thigh.

"Those little girls don't do it for you. A handsome young man like yourself is a little ahead of his peers."

"Huh?" I sit up, suddenly, feeling way too hot under my shirt. It is definitely time to go home.

She puts her hand on my thigh, fingers firmly pressing down. "Did you ever do it in school?"

There is a pause while she stares into my eyes, and I try to remember exactly how much she had to drink at the bar while trying to figure out how the hell I can get out of there, and if it would be okay to be rude since I will probably never talk to her again.

But then she laughs, taking her hand off my thigh, and leans back on the couch. "I'm just kidding—take it easy!"

I laugh awkwardly, as if I knew it was a joke, and shift a bit in my seat, trying to get a couple more inches of space between us.

"I really should go."

"Why? What's the matter, don't you like me?"

What? Does she think I'm blind?

"It's not that, I mean, of course, I like you, it's just that I don't know if it's a good idea for me to be here." I am feeling guilty. I am feeling nervous. I am feeling very tense.

"You're going to leave me here all by myself? Like your brother does?"

I have no idea what to say to that, I just know that every alarm in my head is going off and telling me to get out. I can barely look into her eyes for more than a second or two at a time. It is almost like she is creating this vortex between them, and if I maintain contact, I won't be able to break it, and I will get sucked in somewhere inside those endless lashes and the brilliant green, never to emerge again. Her fingers trace the line of my cheekbone, but I still can't bring myself to look her in the eye.

"Are you okay?" she asks softly.

I just nod, looking away.

"Will. Over here."

She gently grabs my chin with her hand, turning my head toward her.

"What's going on?"

"Nothing. Nothing, I swear."

"Will, what's going on? Please talk to me."

Her eyes keep trying to find mine as mine keep themselves firmly fixed on the floor, until she leans over to run her lips over mine. She kisses me harder as I can't help responding, my tongue in her mouth, our teeth and lips pushing against each other. Her arm slides around my waist, her hand under my shirt, my heart racing—until I remember everything and pull away.

"I'm sorry, I can't. I can't. I'm sorry."

I get up off the bed and start to move toward the door.

"Come back here!" She grabs my shirt with her hand, pulling me suddenly back onto the bed. I fall against her, and she laughs as she wraps her arms around me.

"You can't just leave like that! Please. Tell me what's going on, Will."

"What's going on? It's not obvious?"

"No. No, it's not obvious."

"Alex, you're dating my brother. Isn't he going to be upset about this?"

"Upset about what?" She laughs. "Nothing's happened—yet." She laughs again.

"I'm serious, Alex. I think I need to go."

I still can't remember how much she'd had to drink, but it seems like she'd probably been drinking for a while, and I definitely had not had enough to drink to be doing this kind of thing.

"Where are you going to go?"

"I'm going to go home."

"Oh, come on, don't leave me alone." She runs one long perfect finger across my thigh.

"Alex. Seriously. This is not a good idea. Peter will kill me."

She jerks her hand back. "Why don't you call him then? Call him and get his permission—I think he's over at Maria's house fucking her."

"What? Are you serious? His German tutor?"

"She's teaching him a couple extra things." She laughs dryly. "You know about that. I know you know about that."

"I don't, I don't know anything."

"Yes, you do." She leans over to whisper in my ear, "You hear them. Just like you hear us."

"What? I don't know what you're talking about." I wonder if my face is as red as it felt. I know my palms are sweating.

"I know that you listen, it's okay, I kind of like it."

"You do?"

"Next time, try not to bump your head into the doorknob so much. It makes it kind of obvious." She laughs again at that, loud and clear, and I stare at the inside of her mouth. Part of me wants to crawl into it, and part of me wants to crawl into a hole and die.

"I do NOT."

She laughs again. "Well, I hope it's you, because it helps me get off. Just between you and me, your brother isn't very good, but his naughty little brother—you're so naughty, listening to us."

"I help you get off?" My head can't even begin to process any of this, and my body has never felt so tight.

"Yes. I imagine you on the other side of the door, touching yourself, thinking about me . . . Is that how it happens?"

"I told you, I'm not on the other side of the door!" Part of me still wants to run, but I can't get myself away from her. I can't stop.

"You're not . . . ?"

"No. No." I look down. "I'm in my room."

"And?"

"And yes, sometimes I touch myself when I hear you."

I don't know if I will ever be able to look her in the face again.

"Really?" She sounds delighted. "Really?"

"Yes."

I am still wondering if I did the right thing by telling her, if I should have left an hour ago, if I should never have met her— or if I should just fuck it all and kiss her.

"Have you ever seen us?"

"Seen you? You mean—"

"Seen us fucking. Have you? I left the door open a few times . . ."

"Um . . ." I know I will never be able to look her in the eyes again. "Uh, there was one time, when you guys were on the couch together. I'm sorry. I didn't mean to see."

She slips one hand underneath my chin and forces my face up, so that I have to look her in the eyes. I stare at her nose.

"Do you like kissing? Your brother doesn't."

"What?" I can't help looking into her eyes.

"I haven't been kissed in ages."

"Peter doesn't like kissing?"

"You know how he is—ha, actually, maybe you don't! Yeah, he likes to stick it in, finish his business, and go to sleep."

"But, uh, I thought everyone liked kissing, as long as it was with the right person?" I feel like an idiot listening to words coming out of my mouth.

"I don't know what kissing is like anymore."

By this point, I am staring at her lips, at the luscious red glittering with bits of lip gloss, and wondering how the hell Peter could resist them.

"Will you show me?"

Oh God. Oh God. All I want to do is kiss this girl, and all I can think about is Peter and what kind of a beating I will get if he ever finds out.

"I don't know, are you sure it's okay?"

"If you don't, I will simply shrivel up and die!" She laughs, her hand finding its way back across my thigh.

"I mean, I live with him and all . . ." I feel like my excuses are flimsy, and I'm the only one that seems to care about them.

"Come on. Show me."

I look at her.

The room goes silent. There is some Portishead track on the CD player, but I had long stopped hearing it. I can't hear anything but the pounding in my head. I am aware of my body. I am aware of the couch against me. I am aware of her. Her, her, her.

Her mouth inches from mine, her thighs even closer, her hands on the couch, and there is no reason why my hands aren't touching hers, no reason why I don't have a hand on her thigh. Her skin is so close I can see the fine blond hairs but still I am not touching it—for no reason at all except that I'm scared. I can't make myself move.

"Will."

She slips one hand under my chin and lifts my head up, so I have to look her in the eyes. I make contact for a second before looking away.

How desperately I want this girl, and how that desperation scares the shit out of me and makes me want to run to the safety of my room, to the safety of my comic books and my records and my music and my quiet, quiet, quiet life. How I wish I'd never met her. How I wish my stomach wasn't in knots, my sweat on my hands, how I wish I hadn't met this person who makes me feel nervous and small and stupid and awkward and yet utterly consumed with desire.

I try to stand up.

"Will. Stay." She grabs my arm, pulling me back down on the bed. "Is something wrong? Did I say something wrong? I didn't mean to make you uncomfortable—I'm sorry—I just really want to kiss you, and you are so beautiful, I couldn't help it. I thought it might make you want to kiss me, too. I'm sorry. That dream I had? The one I told you about? It wasn't a dream. It's been my fantasy ever since I first saw you. I'm sorry. Maybe

I shouldn't have said anything. I just didn't know what to say, and I just wanted you to want me like I want you."

There is a pause.

"If you don't want to, it's really okay. We can go back to the bar, we can have a drink, we can listen to music, whatever you like. I'm sorry I said the wrong things."

I can't believe it. Her voice has gotten so soft, so hesitant, I can't believe this is the same girl. There is nothing about this that feels real. Nothing. At. All. We sit awkwardly for a moment, then, just as I am about to move my left hand to her right thigh, she takes a deep breath and stands up.

"Okay then," she says in a forced cheerful voice, "where shall we go? What do you want to do?"

"Alex. Alex." I kicked the words out. "I would like to kiss you."

"What?" She stares at me. "You do?" The grin shoots across her face, and if I thought her eyes had been bright before, now they are brilliant. I can't help smiling back at her.

"Yeah. Come here." I grab her hand and pull her back onto the couch.

Laughing, she falls on top of me, her legs on either side of mine, her lips against my face, and, before I have time to think—my tongue is in her mouth, her tongue is in mine, and everything disappears while I feel her skin and her breath, and she is closer to me than I'd ever imagined possible, and I try to wrap myself around her, while she presses herself against me, and we kiss and kiss and kiss—until she pulls herself back.

Did I do something wrong?

"Wow, you really know what you're doing."

"I do?"

"Yeah. You just got me so wet."

This time, I know I'm turning bright red.

"Wanna feel it?"

She takes my right hand in hers and slips it between her legs. Even through her underwear, I can tell how wet she is. I am so mesmerized, I don't even notice that she lets go of my hand. I am too busy moving my fingers back and forth, in delicious strokes, marveling at the warm wetness that I am finally allowed to feel. I have wanted to touch her for so long, I can't even remember when I didn't.

She is starting to breathe heavily, her hips moving against my hand, pressing into me, and I am losing myself in the rhythm of the moment, until she whispers, "Those panties are getting in the way, aren't they?"

I look up, startled. She is grinning at me. I smile back. "Want me to take them off for you?"

"Yes."

Feeling like I am living the life of someone else, I slip them off with a smoothness I never knew I had, as if I have been taking off girls' underwear every day of my life.

"Oh, look at that! They're so wet!"

She grabs them out of my hand and brings them up to her

nose. She sniffs delicately before holding them out to me. "Want to smell?"

I grin. I have never met anyone like this before in my life. I am in a movie. This is not real.

"Sure, okay."

She passes them over to me, and I let the smell pull me in—dark, musty, rich, sweet. I just breathe, then, for a second, I wonder if she will notice if I take them home.

"Okay, okay!" She flings the underwear on the floor. "Pay attention to me now!" Grabbing my shirt, she pulls me on top of her.

"Now what about you?" she pants, rubbing her body against mine.

"What about me? What do you mean, what about me?"

"What's in there?" she asks, slipping her hand between our two bodies, running it down between my legs, pressing against my zipper, pressing against me. "I can feel it. I want to see it."

Without a second thought, I reach down, unzip my pants, and slide them off. I'm so hard, I'm almost embarrassed by how obvious is my desire.

"Oh my," she says, smiling. "You're lovely. You're so big and hard and pretty and thick."

I am blushing. I want to hide. I wish it were darker in the room.

"You are the perfect length."

Part of me wants to pull my pants back up, and part of me

wants her to touch it more than I have ever wanted anything. If I feel any more conflict, I might split in half and fall through the floor.

"Can I touch it?"

I want those perfect lip-glossed lips. I want those smooth fingers. I want her. I want her so much, I don't even know if I can get the words out. And if I get them out, will I sound like I'm begging?

"Yes. Yes. Yes, please."

Her hands are caressing my thighs. She reaches up and wraps a hand around me, making a slow stroke back across my foreskin to reveal the already moist head of my cock. It's warm and hard in her hand. She feels my balls, runs her hand through my pubes, pulls me closer, and I can't believe any of this is real. I can't believe this is my life.

I am spacing out. I am dreaming. My cock feels like stone. This is not real, until—I feel a warm lick across the head of my cock, then another, and, like a warm glove, her mouth gently slides on. I look down. I look down at her blond hair, at her lips around my cock, at her hands. I look down, I see it, and I still can't believe it's really happening. I would never have predicted it, not in a million years—not this girl, not me, not here, not now.

"You don't have to—" I awkwardly stammer. I feel guilty.

"What? Are you kidding?" She looks up at me with shock. "I've been dreaming about this forever. Just enjoy it, and let me."

Her mouth slides back onto me, she's got almost all of me in her mouth, and then my cock is in her hand, and she's licking my balls, and I have never felt anything so perfect.

She moves back up, we kiss some more, my cock pressing against her stomach. She bends it down and slips it between her legs. I am getting very nervous. Her hands are all over my body.

Before I realize what's happening, she slips me inside her. With almost as quick a gesture, she takes off her top. Her nipples are hard. I reach for them.

"A little harder," she says softly, in my ear. "Come on. Take me. I'll let you know if it's too much."

"I don't want to hurt you."

"Just keep going. It's okay, baby."

I let go. I start rubbing her with one hand, pushing myself against her, licking her breasts, kissing her face.

"Don't stop," she pants. "Harder."

I press and push and pull on her breasts. I think of all those times I saw her with Peter, all those times I saw her walk through my house in a towel, all those times I'd stared at her and wondered what she would feel like, what she would smell like, what she would taste like—I remember it all, and it makes me want her more than ever.

She takes her right hand and pulls my cock close to her, rubbing my stiff head against her clit, but I'm too tall, the position is wrong, we can't get it in, so she pushes me down onto the sofa. I'm sitting, and she straddles me, one hand pressed against the wall to keep her balance, the other spreading her pussy lips apart for me. Slowly, slowly, she pushes her way in, lowering herself on top of me, breasts in my face. I begin to suck on her nipples, my hands on her ass, pulling her tight. She begins to ride me, long, wet strokes up and down my full length. I'm deep inside of her, I can feel every ridge on my penis, every inch, moving inside of her. She pushes against me. I can't believe how much of me fits inside her. How wet and warm she feels. How perfect the rhythm. I squeeze her tits with my hand, sucking on her pink nipples, while her thighs slam against my legs—until she gets off me.

"Is everything okay?" I panic. Did I do something wrong?

"It's okay, honey," she says, running one wet finger across my lips. "Shh. I just want to see you, to taste you, covered with me."

She leans forward and takes me deep into her mouth. I can't believe it. Then she turns around, her ass facing me, and re-mounts, putting her hands down on the floor, riding my cock. I can see, I can watch, my glistening shaft going in and out of her, going in and out of her lovely pale ass.

"Oh God, Will, I'm going to come," she pants.

I've never heard that before. I mean, not in real life, at least. I can feel my own cum building in my cock. I struggle to push her off, but she only slams down on me more.

"It's okay, it's okay, don't stop."

She starts to moan, and I lose it. I can feel myself spasming inside her, the warmth of my cum filling her up, while she presses herself down harder. I start to feel light-headed. My cum is leaking out between her legs. She slides off me. I start to stand up, but she pushes me back down, taking me in her mouth one more time.

"You thought I wouldn't clean you up?"

I can't believe it, but then again, I can't believe any of it. I sit back and watch her, and everything feels like fantasy and reality at the same time, and I can't wait to see what happens next.

Rick

I remember the first time I let Rick have my feet.

The first time we met, I never expected anything to happen between us. We'd met at a party, through mutual friends, and only managed a decent conversation. I wasn't interested in him, I actually forgot about him pretty quickly, and the feeling seemed mutual—at least until he stopped by.

"Hey, uh, it's Rick. I . . . , uh, I met you at Tracy's party? I live over on Sixth Street?"

"Yes, right, okay." As I was trying to remember him, I was also trying to remember if I'd told him my address.

"I just wondered if you needed anything."

I laughed. "No," I told him, "but thank you." I started to close the door.

"Please," he said, "But I'd like to do something. Do

you have dry cleaning you need picked up? Laundry? I'm right around the corner, it really wouldn't be a problem."

"Rick. I've got no dry cleaning to be picked up, no laundry to be done. I'm okay. Really."

We stared at each other in silence as he looked at me imploringly, and I wondered what the hell to make of this situation.

"Do you think I could rub your feet? I'd really love to do that for you."

There was a pause, a long pause, while I thought that one through. This was unexpected. My first reaction was the normal one—a bit of shock, a bit of outrage, a bit of revulsion, some kind of moral indignation, a bit of what the fuck—but then I decided it wouldn't be so awful.

"I've got twenty dollars," he said. "I will give you twenty dollars if you let me rub your feet."

That killed any hesitation I might have had.

"Okay, fine, okay . . . We can do it in the bedroom," I said, leading the way.

Rick quickly situated himself on the floor, reverently taking my right foot in both his hands, and began to rub. Slowly, he caressed my arch, my ankle, my big toe, my heel—touching each part gently, deeply, stroking and pressing the skin.

His fingers ran delicately over my foot, as I let myself get lost in the sensation. My shoulders and neck were just starting to relax, my back unwinding, my body falling deeper into the softness of the bed, when, all of a sudden I was jerked awake by my left leg slipping off the bed, falling naturally downward, and abruptly touching something hot and hard. My eyes opened, my foot jerked back in shock; I knew what it was that I had just felt, and I wished desperately that I hadn't felt it, or at least that he hadn't noticed I had felt it.

While his tongue and lips delicately explored my right foot, and I tried not to think about what I'd just discovered, Rick raised his right hand and slipped it around my ankle. Moving so slowly that it seemed almost interminable, the grip of his hand tightened, his lips left my toes, and his tongue ran its away over the arch of my foot, underneath it, above it, and across to my ankle.

As his right hand made its way around my knee, just grazing the bottom of my thigh, I could feel the ache between my legs start to grow, my mind painfully aware both of the proximity of his fingers to my pussy and the seemingly infinite distance from one to the other. As long as his fingers weren't inside me, they were awfully far away. I willed them closer, but they just lingered on my knee, Rick apparently distracted by the actions of his tongue around my toes.

Very cautiously, I stretched out my left foot, inch by inch, straining to determine, with my eyes closed and my head still flat on the bed, exactly where my foot was in relation to his thighs, his legs, and his crotch. A few seconds later, I hit the warm, comforting muscular mass of his thigh. It didn't take long until I began snaking my foot along the thigh, inch by inch, until I hit his hip. I ran my big toe along the edge and slipped my way over. I knew that I got to what I'd been looking for when I felt the bulging lines of his cock, and Rick stopped licking to exhale a hot breath over the edge of my foot. Success.

I began gently rubbing my foot over his pants, feeling his gratifying pressure in exchange. Just as I'd hoped, after less than a minute his hand rediscovered my knee. His fingers released their hold and began making their way up my thigh. I wondered how long it would take him to reach the wetness that had been seeping out from between my legs and what he would do when he got there.

I didn't find out. His hand stopped moving about halfway up my thigh. I lay back on the bed, my eyes staring at the ceiling— it seemed inconceivable, but his attention was still focused on my foot. His fingers mere inches from my pussy, they were oblivious to its presence, his energies still directed at my toes, ankle, and heel. This was truly bizarre, on numerous levels.

My thoughts were interrupted by Rick's pulling back, away from my foot. I lifted my head to look at him.

"Do you think," he said, "if I paid a little extra, I could see more?"

I just stared at him. I had no idea what he was talking about. I'd forgotten I was getting paid for this.

He must have thought that I was just holding out for the bigger bucks. "I'll give you another twenty?"

"You'll give me another twenty to see what?"

"You know," and here he gestured at his shirt.

Feeling the mood of the moment, I very slowly and seductively peeled off my top. Rick's eyes got bigger. I slid my foot back between his legs. The guy must have been in pain, he was pressing so hard against the seam of his pants.

"Why don't you unzip your pants?" I suggested.

He blinked at me, startled.

"It's okay. Take 'em off."

"What? Are you sure? Is that okay?"

"Rick. Take them off."

"Yes, ma'am," he replied, as he quickly stood up and fumbled with his zipper, hurrying before I could change my mind. The boxers on the floor, it was my turn to stare. He was massive—huge, engorged, sticking straight out with desire.

I smiled at him, stretching my foot back in his direction. That move was just as effective as if I'd barked orders at him—Rick instantly knelt again on the floor, grabbing my foot with his hands, and went back to work.

I couldn't resist. "Come up here on the bed."

"What?" Rick looked up at me, startled, mouth still around my big toe.

"Get up here," I replied, patting the bed next to me.

Ever dutiful, Rick let go of my leg and came to sit awkwardly on the edge of the bed next to me.

"No. I want you to lie down with your head over there." I pointed at the far end of the bed. "And I'm going to lie down with my head over here." I pointed at the other end of the bed.

"Okay," he said, quickly adjusting himself according to my instructions.

"Good. Okay." I lay down and placed my foot in his hands. Beginning to understand, although clearly still baffled by his elevated status, Rick started to rub. Whatever he'd done in the past, it had obviously never extended to this, but I was okay with it. I enjoyed making him uncomfortable.

I gave him a couple of minutes to adjust to his new position, waiting until I could tell that he had become absorbed in his task. Then I made my move.

"Don't stop," I told him.

I ran my hand over his thigh to his hip. Every time Rick paused, so did I. As soon as he started up again, so did I.

It didn't take long for me to get where I was going. This guy was hard. I could feel practically every vein bulging out along the skin, full of blood and heat and desire. I started by stroking back and forth with my thumb, my other fingers just pressed against the skin. Again, every time Rick stopped, so did I.

After a few minutes of rubbing (by Rick) and stroking (by me), I began to move my whole hand, gently shifting the skin back and forth, slowly building up pressure and speed. I was rewarded with a huge shudder and a massive exhalation.

"Keep rubbing," I told him. "If you stop, so do I."

You wouldn't think one girl's foot could be so interesting, but Rick acted as though it was the only one he'd ever seen. Desperate to keep me moving, he licked and rubbed and stroked every inch of it, but he didn't stand a chance.

I felt the pressure of his hands decrease as the pressure of mine increased. It didn't take long for his hands to stop moving completely, his thighs clenching and all the blood in his body racing between his legs. I allowed him about thirty seconds, waiting until the thrusting of his hips indicated that I was moments away from losing him.

And then I stopped.

I kept my hand wrapped around his cock, but I wasn't moving anymore.

"Oh, please, please," he moaned. "Don't stop."

"Don't tell me what to do," I snapped at him.

Suddenly aware of what he'd done, Rick began apologizing, but I cut him off—that part didn't turn me on. "It's okay. This time."

"Do you want me to keep rubbing?" he asked.

"No. We're going to do something else," I said. "Stand up. We're going to the kitchen."

"Okay." He leapt up and reached for his boxers.

"Nope. Leave those there. We're not done yet."

He was confused, and I knew this would be priceless. When we got to the kitchen, I pointed at my sink.

"Do you see those dishes?"

He nodded.

"I'd like you to wash them. After you've washed them, we can go back to the bedroom."

Rick looked at me, trying to figure out exactly what I was getting at.

"Wash them," I ordered.

Rick scuttled over to the sink, grabbed a sponge in one hand, a dirty plate in another, and started scrubbing.

I just stood and watched. It was a beautiful sight. This massively muscular man was standing at my sink, washing my dishes, naked from the waist down, his huge, swollen cock still sticking straight out.

Funny the things we don't know about ourselves until life helps us accidentally discover them. Up until then, my sex life had been pretty straightforward, and nothing, nothing had turned me on as much as the events of this afternoon. I could feel the ache inside, the wetness drenching my pussy, the electric tingle on my skin—I loved this feeling of control, I loved seeing the look of pathetic lust in his eyes, the subservient little face he kept making, anxious to satisfy. I felt in charge. I felt powerful and beautiful and sexy.

I waited until his hardness started to recede, until its angle was more seventy degrees than a perfect ninety, and I walked over to the sink.

"Don't stop," I told him, as I wrapped my fingers around his cock. "And don't you dare break a dish."

Standing right next to the poor boy as he desperately tried to hold on to the plates in the soapy water, I kept my breathing cool as I began to rub. Faster, harder—it wasn't long until he was back at ninety degrees.

"Oh God," he moaned as the sponge dropped to the bottom of the sink, one hand gripping the faucet, the other the edge of the sink.

"Rick. You're not done yet."

There were still two plates left in the sink. With a deep sigh as he tried to maintain self-control, Rick slowly released his grip on the edge of the sink and grabbed one of the plates. I started rubbing again.

Just as the second plate was neatly placed on the drying rack, Rick moving with incredible precision in a desperate attempt not to break anything, I could see the telltale droplets of precum forming on the edge of his cock. Perfect timing.

I let go. "Good job. Thanks for doing the dishes."

Rick just panted a bit, wringing the towel dry as though his life depended on it.

I gave him a second. "You can put the towel down."

He put the towel down reluctantly and turned to me, his hands resting uncertainly on the edge of the sink.

I turned and walked into the bedroom, Rick eagerly at my heels.

Within moments, we were right back where we'd been—his tongue on my ankle, his fingers on my heel, my hand around his cock. I started to rub, gently at first, then with increasing pressure. His tongue ran over my foot, around my toe, up the arch and across the ankle. I gently rubbed his balls, leaning over just enough to send my tongue gently skipping over them as Rick gave a huge sigh, releasing his hold on my foot ever so slightly. Before I could take my mouth away from his dick, Rick sensed my disapproval and grabbed hold again. We were back on track.

I deliberately tormented him—picking up the pace just long enough for his hips to start mimicking my movements before switching to slow and deep—unrelentingly keeping him on the edge of orgasm, but never doing it long enough to let him get there. I didn't care about the foot rub; that wasn't the part that turned me on. The part that turned me on was watching him struggle to keep his attentions focused as I coaxed him higher and higher to a peak of intense sexual need.

I waited until the next time I had him on the edge, then, just before slowing down, I stopped completely.

"Hey, Rick?"

"Wha—huh," he panted, fumbling as he tried to sit up, the blood rushing back to his head.

"Don't sit up," I said, as I pushed him back down onto the bed. "You don't have to move. I just wanted to tell you something. I've got a new idea."

"Okay—what's that?"

"Before you finish—and you will finish—you've got to ask my permission."

"Uh, okay."

"It's not a big deal, just, you know, when you feel yourself about to come, just say, 'Mistress, may I come?' That's all. And then, if I tell you it's okay, you can go ahead, and if I say no, then, well, you can't." I paused. "Got that?"

There was a silence as his brain processed the information.

"Will you really let me finish?"

"Yes, yes, I will."

"Oh, that would be great." The surprise, relief, and gratification in his voice was obvious. "Thank you so much." His hands clutched mine gratefully. I shook myself free.

"You don't have to thank me—just ask my permission before you do."

"Got it."

"Good," I replied, and resumed my rubbing. This time I was focused on getting him to finish, or at least at getting him to the point of having to ask my permission, so I kept my motions quick and shallow. It didn't take long.

"Mistre—Mistre—Oh God, I think—I'm about—I'm, uh, oh God, Mistress, I'm about to come—"

With as much of a curt, businesslike tone as I could muster, I said, "Sorry, Rick, not time yet," releasing my grip on his cock.

"Oh God," he said, shuddering, grabbing for my hands. I kept them neatly out of reach. "Is there something I can do for you? Please. What can I do? Please, Mistress, what can I do?"

I thought for a moment. I honestly didn't want this to go on all day. As fun as it was, it was going to get old quickly.

"Just keep rubbing," I told him, as I gently started up again. This time, I let him get hard and full—and I didn't let up. I didn't slow down. I didn't change my pace. I kept my movements constant and my rhythm precise.

Before long, we were back there again.

"Mistre—Mistress, oh God, please, I'm about, oh can I, oh—"

I stopped my movements but kept my hand gripped. "Sorry Rick, what were you saying?"

He took a deep breath. "Mistress, please, I'm about to come. Please, Mistress, please let me finish." The puppy dog was begging.

Ever obliging, I relented. "Sure, Rick, you can come."

My hand started moving again as I built him up to an impeccable climax. Less than thirty seconds later, Rick's entire body tensed up, the hot breath stopped hitting the sole of my foot, everything silent, and then, with a huge heaving moan, the cum shot out of his cock and all over his stomach. It was a beautiful moment. I let go and smiled.

"Don't forget to leave your forty dollars," I said cruelly, jolting him out of his postorgasmic daze.

"Of course, of course," he stammered, pulling the bills out of his wallet as he hurried to put his clothes on—anxious not to overstay his welcome.

I lay on the bed, watching him dress. When he was ready, we stared at each other for a moment.

"Here you go, mistress," he murmured meekly, handing me two twenty-dollar bills.

I took them as I got up off the bed.

"Thank you," I replied politely before shoving him against the wall, my lips inches from his hips, my hands on his chest. I spoke slowly. "No one can find out what happened here today. But if you keep your mouth shut, like the good little boy I know you are, I'll see you back here tomorrow at three o'clock—got that?"

He nodded, and I let him leave—for now.

Electricity

Today was one of those days where I really wanted to lie in bed with someone. For some reason, the space inside my upper thighs felt especially naked, especially empty, without someone's hands to touch them. I craved fingers running reconnaissance missions, exploring the territory before the tongue would take its turn.

I don't always mind being alone—it's not like I lie awake at night wondering when I'll find someone to kiss me while I sleep. It's not like I go out to bars and explore the crowds, searching for a face to wake up next to. It's not like that at all.

I go out by myself, and I'm used to it. I like it. I can come when I want, leave when I want, and I don't have to do favors for anybody. I can be selfish and secretive, and no one gets mad. I even like going to movies alone, where I can watch all the credits (if I want) or leave early (if I want), and I don't have to ruin that moment at the end of the movie, where your head is still lost in the lives of the people you just watched on the big screen, by making conversation about where to go next.

I don't have to call if I'm running late, I don't have to clean up until I'm ready, and if I feel like dressing ugly, no one minds.

I'm independent, and it suits me fine, except on days like today, where my bed feels awfully big for just one girl, and I wish there would be a knock at the door, and I would open it to see you standing there.

"Hello," I would say.

"Hello," you would say.

And then you would take my hand and lead me to the bedroom, where we would get in bed together, and you would wrap your arms around me and slip one hand between my thighs, and we would just lie there and feel each other's skin. I would breathe in and out, matching my breath to the rise and fall of your chest, my hand tracing the lines of your ribs, then working up the courage to run down your stomach, before slipping my way to your hips. I would rest there for a moment, feeling the crevice just behind the front of your pelvis. My fingers would trace that hollow while my ears listened to the sound of your heart, and I pressed my hips even closer against you.

While I drew figure eights along your hips, your breath would slowly speed up, each inhale growing more shallow, each exhale

coming faster, and I could feel your thighs stiffening with anticipation. While I kept tracing numbers, your fingers, still between
my thighs, would start to move higher, slowly, gently, while my
wetness seeped lower, running between my legs, until it found
your fingers, and you sighed with pleasure.

I would give in to curiosity and let my fingers drift over the
edge of your thighs until I found your cock, incredibly hard and
amazingly smooth at the same time. Upon contact, my inhala-
tion matched yours, fingers marveling at the perfect softness of
your skin. I started to rub my hand up and down, the skin almost like liquid, shifting perfectly under my hand, pulling up
just enough over the head before pressing down at the base of
the shaft. My hand moved faster, like a machine, the skin slipping and sliding like some exquisite fabric, while your breath
and my breath quickened in tandem, the speed of our breath in
direct correlation to the speed of my hand.

While breath and hand pressed and pulled and slipped and
slid, your hand would find itself drawn by my wetness deeper
between my legs until it found the dark hot source and, with
mutual sighs, you would shove one, then two, fingers inside me
as my thighs arched around your arm in response.

Not realizing how empty I had been until you filled me, you
fit perfectly into my insides, sending rivers of electric pleasure
along every inch of my body. The only sensation more acute
was the one caused by your other hand as it pressed against my
lower back, your nails digging slightly into my skin, making my

flesh feel like a million sensors overloaded by the voltage of your touch.

The power of having you near, the energy of your closeness, the current of your desire, would light me up like an overdecorated Christmas tree, my skin seemingly on fire, my body aching for you to press deeper, push harder, while my hand moved faster and faster over your cock, the skin so smooth, so soft, so delicate, that the very act of moving it back and forth would hypnotize me.

Lulled by the rhythm of my motion, by the pattern of your breath, by the warmth rising from you, by the delicious electricity of your fingers within my body, I could feel myself lost in my own mind, the confines of my body slipping away from me, the only real gravity dictated by the energy of my insides and the energy of yours. Lost in the sensation, I thought of nothing else, I felt nothing else, but the rhythm of my hand on your cock and your fingers inside me.

In and out, in and out—every time your fingers pulled out, I wanted nothing more than to feel them inside again. Every time your fingers pushed in, I wanted nothing more than the delicious anticipation of having them rest on the rim of my entrance, in that split second where you waited, perhaps teasing me, perhaps just lost in your own heady sensations while my hand brought you closer and closer to your fantasies, to a gorgeous climax of your own.

Then you would lean over and begin to run your tongue

across my breasts, your teeth lightly biting my nipples, the pleasure and pain mingling into one wave of pure perfect sensation, and it would be almost too much for me to stand. When you began to breathe over my skin, your hot breath cascading over the freshly damp flesh, then I feared I might short-circuit—too much power, too much voltage, over a limited system.

Desperate to finish you so that I could lose myself in your touch, desperate to finish you so that you would stop touching me for one instant, and I could remember how to breathe, I accelerated my pace. I shifted my machine into a higher gear, my rhythm steadily increasing, until your only movement was a tensing in the thighs and a faster rise and fall of the chest. Your hand resting between my legs but without moving—you lay there beside me, moaning slightly as your climax came closer and closer and closer until it was there, and your hand grabbed my thigh while your voice begged me not to stop, and I leaned over and slid my hand over your cock, just in time to catch the stream of cum and to feel the pulsing of your veins against my lips.

Then it was my turn.

After resting for a moment, while we both lay against each other, matching our breaths, lulled by the rhythm of our lungs, your fingers slowly made their way back between my legs, drawn deeper by the pressure of my hips against your hand. I could feel how swollen I was, and I knew how slippery I must feel. With delicate precision, made all the more precise by your postorgasmic calm, you began making little perfect circles with your fingers against my clit, and I could feel myself falling into an endless tunnel of pleasure, rocked to a state of almost intoxication by the waves of electric sensation.

All I could think was, "more, more, more," and all I could feel was your hot breath on my breast and your fingers alternating between tracing my clit and fucking me, first with two and then three fingers, filling me up perfectly, precisely, every inch of my skin curving against yours, until the waves consumed me, and I came with a sudden rush that left me unable to breathe while I grabbed you and held you close, close, closer.

Perfect. Sublime. Delicious. Words fled through my brain, each unwilling to stay, but flickering once, in brilliant neon, trying to describe the sensations I was feeling. Incredible. I held on to you, unwilling to let your hands escape me, desperate to keep your breath on my skin, my lungs needing yours to dictate pattern and rhythm. I tried to hold you close, I tried to keep you closer, but the more I grabbed, the less there was to find.

You weren't there. You never were. The bed was empty, and I was alone.

But with my eyes closed, anything could be possible. With my eyes closed, I could make you stay as long as I wanted. With my eyes closed, I breathed deeply to myself, ran fingers across my skin to remind myself of how that could feel, and slid my hand between my legs.

Reaction

The worst part wasn't what he said, it was my reaction.

"I bet you've never been properly fucked," he whispered, liquored breath heavy on my ear.

I should have been outraged. I should have been insulted and offended. And I was. Truly. I even felt a bit ill to my stomach. But I have to be honest—part of me still wanted to ask him to take me home.

"No, I haven't," I couldn't help admitting, even though I knew those were the wrong three words to say.

But why should I deny it? I was sure he'd be too drunk to remember, if he was even sober enough to register what I was saying, and it was the truth. I'd never been properly fucked. Not properly fucked the way I imagined fucking to be. I mean, I'd had sex before, I'd made love before, I'd had tongues and fingers and vibrators, and every body part that is supposed to fit into my body parts had been there—more than several times. I'd had relationships and one-night stands, I'd had affairs and everything a young city girl is supposed to have, although clearly not everything a young city girl might want. I wanted to be properly fucked.

I'd never realized it before that moment. I'd never thought about it. I'd never felt like I was missing something, until right then, and then I ached for it. I wanted it so badly, I couldn't believe the depth of my desire. How had I never noticed this before? Where did it come from and why because of this alcohol-reeking man whose eyes were still, somehow, bright and blue?

I wanted someone, I wanted him, to take me home and to make me forget who I was. I wanted to get lost in a moment that would feel like the movies, which would make me hot and sweaty and satisfied, but only for that second before I would be desperate for more, even when I knew that more might split me in two.

Wouldn't that be rapturous?

Pressed up against the wall, hands everywhere, tongues everywhere, thoughts nowhere.

I looked at his eyes and his dirty hair under a green baseball cap, and part of me wondered if I would be able to live with myself if I went home with him.

While another part of me wondered if he'd even been serious.

But most of me knew I wouldn't do anything about it, even if he had been. Nice girls don't respond to comments like that.

Nice girls don't go home with boys that leer and talk about fucking. Nice girls wait for nice boys, and when they don't turn up, nice girls go home alone.

Which is what I did. As usual.

I arrived home exhausted. Dirty. Sweaty. It had been a long day, a long night, a long week. I'd played a show that had gone on longer than most. I'd rolled around on the floor and done the usual microphone antics, and I just needed to take a bath and go to bed. I could feel my body sticky, and I knew every inch reeked of cigarette smoke.

The water was almost too hot—the way I like it. The tub was deep—the way I like it. The steam rose off the water, coating the parts of my body that weren't under water in a fine layer of condensation—the way I like it. I lay back, feeling the warm water holding me, surrounding me, enveloping me. I slipped down into the water until my head was the only part still exposed to air.

I ran my fingers across the edge of the water, slicing it, watching the ripples undulate out, rocking against my skin, against the porcelain walls of the bathtub, water versus air, water versus skin, water versus wall, solid versus fluid, one against the other, the other against the one, and somewhere, in the midst of it all, my body, my flesh, my skin, my physical substance filling up space in the water, in the air, covered with water, with steam, with sweat . . .

Slipping farther down, I let the water rush over my face. Feeling myself completely contained, like an embryo, I floated, trying to separate from my body, from my space, from the water, from the air, losing myself in the water, not anywhere, not somewhere, but just there, losing my body, just feeling my thoughts, my needs, my desire.

The water touched me. It knocked against me. I felt a part of it. I came up in a sudden upward movement, gasping for air. I felt it fill me. I felt the cool air against my skin that seemed shocked by the exposure. I slid back down, keeping just enough of my face above the water to breathe, and closed my eyes.

I thought of those blue eyes. I thought of his dirty blond hair. I ignored the alcohol. I ignored the leer. I thought of his hands and his fingers. I remembered what his arms had looked like, the freckled skin, the early summer tan, and I took a deep breath as the water rocked around me.

What would it be like to let him fuck me? To let him touch me? What did he think when he looked at me? What had he seen that made him talk to me in that way? What was his fantasy? What would he do with me if I were there, in bed with him, naked and willing?

Would he run his tongue along my skin? Would he get violent? Would he bite my breasts and leave little bruises along my skin? Would he run fingernails across my arms or would he just grab them and hold them and pull me close, the skin pressed tightly under his grip? Would he fuck me lying down or standing up or kneeling like a dog? Would he fuck me against the wall or in the bed? Would he pull my hair or run his teeth along my ear? How would he touch me? Would there be love there? Desire? Domination? How would I feel? Would it touch parts of me that would cry out for more, or would I just cry out and beg him to stop?

Would we do it once or again and again?

Would it hurt or would it feel good?

Would I see him again? Or would he break me once and have his fill?

The water embraced my skin as my fingers slipped between my legs, and I lost myself in my own imagination, wondering about the danger of desiring what you are afraid to have—or is it precisely the danger that makes the desire so intoxicating?

I kept running my fingers across my clit, inside my body, along my thighs and my breasts, but I just made myself more and more frustrated. I couldn't make myself come. I couldn't finish. I just got hotter as I felt myself growing more swollen and more frustrated and more irritable, the gentle water mocking me and my failed attempts, and I couldn't fucking come. My fantasies kept starting out strong, full of manly hands and sexual domination, desire and control and lust, and then they'd fade as I kept remembering I was just one girl alone in a tub, and where will that ever get you?

I had to find out. I rose up, out of the water, dripping across the floor, and went straight for the phone.

"Kathryn, I need Tim's number."

"What? Tim? I didn't know you two knew each other. Tim from down the street?"

"Yeah. I want to call him."

"You know each other?"

"I just met him tonight. I want to call him. Can I get his number?"

Her tone changed. She laughed. "You liiiiiiike him!"

"Oh, shut up." I was not in the mood for this. "Can I just have his number? Please?"

She knew when to be quick. "Sure. Yes. I'll get it for you."

Several seconds later, I stood in the hallway, still naked, still dripping, shivering slightly in the hallway draft, listening to the ringing of a not-too-distant phone, and feeling like an idiot. I slammed the receiver down. What was I thinking? What would I possibly say?

"Hi Tim, it's Sarah. Do you still want to fuck me?"

God, what a moron. What was wrong with me? What was wrong with women, in general, that we would want to get treated this way? That we would be turned on by being treated in this way? I had issues. Clearly.

I went to bed. Irritated and frustrated.

And yet, despite my good intentions and common sense, I couldn't stop thinking about Tim. I'd be in the shower, and I'd feel his hands rough against my hips. I'd be standing in line at the supermarket, and I'd hear his voice whispering in my ear, "let me show you what it's like to be fucked." I'd be driving my car, and I'd imagine his hand running under my skirt. I'd imagine him telling me to get off the road, to pull over, to turn the engine off, to get in the backseat. I'd get into bed at night, and I'd fall asleep to images of him on top of me, behind me, his tongue on my skin, his teeth on my breasts, and I'd wake up in the morning to find my hand between my legs.

But I still couldn't make myself come.

I'd hear his voice, "let me show you what it's like to be fucked," and I could feel myself getting wet. I'd leak into my best pants at work. I'd stain my skirt sitting in the car. I'd excuse myself and go to the bathroom while at dinner. My nipples were always hard.

It was out of control. I hated it. I couldn't sleep. I just wanted to sit and eat chocolate and will myself out of this sensation, but nothing worked. I just kept using up batteries and driving myself crazy.

I still had his number. It sat by the phone, staring at me, while I waged a battle of will and common sense versus desire.

But it soon became a battle of will and common sense versus insomnia, frustration, irritability, need, and desire.

"Let me show you what it's like to be fucked," became my mantra. I heard it everywhere, but I found it nowhere. I had to call him. I had to call the asshole and let him treat me the way I clearly wanted to be treated.

An educated girl like me. I wanted to get properly fucked. What was wrong with me? I knew better, so why couldn't I stop thinking about him? I wanted him to show me what it was like, and I couldn't stop imagining what that might be.

All right, all bets were off. Let the games begin. No one would ever have to know—except me, I had to know.

"Tim? Do you remember me?"

"Sarah? I'm not sure. Did we meet before?"

"Yeah, yeah, we did. I'm a friend of Kathryn's. We met at the bar last week."

"Oh yeah, that's right. Yeah, sure. Hey. How's it going?"

"It's going well." Actually, it wasn't going well, at all. If he could barely remember me, I was sure he'd never remember what he'd promised to teach me. But what can you do? I'd already gone too far to get out.

"Are you going to be at the bar later tonight?"

"Yeah. Yeah, I'll be there around ten o'clock. You, too?"

"Yeah, perfect. See you there."

I hung up the phone, the receiver slippery with my sweat, my heart beating in my ears, my nipples already hard against my bra. I was a mess. This better be worth it, I thought. This better be good. This better fix something.

The bar was empty when I got there, empty except for Tim, with his half-finished beer in one hand and his next one already waiting, and the bartender, who seemed to be doing the crossword puzzle.

"Hey," I said.

"Hey," he said. "Wanna beer?"

"Yeah. Sure." I figured it would give me a chance to figure out what to say next, and maybe it would help give me the courage actually to say it.

Before I knew it, the beer was in my hand, I was on the stool, and Tim was looking me over, appraisingly.

"You had that show the other night, right?"

"Yeah, I did." I smiled. At least he remembered. "That was me."

He grinned back at me, raising his beer in toast. "Way to go. That shit rocked."

"You liked it?"

"Oh yeah, totally. You were hot, girl." He grinned again. "Not. Bad. At. All."

He winked at me, and I almost spilled my beer. I felt like I'd forgotten my cue cards at home. Was I this out of practice? Part of me wanted to lose all tact and just tell him what I wanted, but I vaguely remembered there being some game one had to play, some dance two partners had to perform, in order to make the complicated transition from point A to point B, from bar to home to bed.

"Whatcha thinking about?" He leaned over, his face inches from mine, his blue eyes almost mesmerizing enough to ignore the smell of beer that seemed to be coming out of his pores. "I can tell you've got something on your mind . . ."

"Me?" I laughed nervously, covering it up with a swig of beer. "Nah. Nothing. Just been a long day, that's all."

"You should drink more." I got another wink. "It's good for ya, you know. Want another drink?"

"No, no, that's okay. I've got a lot left with this one."

He grinned at me again. "All right then. Just give me a shout when you're ready."

And with that, to my shock and dismay, he turned around to watch the football game on the television.

This was not going right at all. I downed my beer as quickly as I could. Liquid courage, is that what they call alcohol?

"Hey, Tim."

"Yeah?" He spun slowly around in his stool, keeping his eyes on the screen for as long as possible before transferring them to my nervous face.

"I, uh, was wondering if you'd mind walking me home?"

"You're leaving now?" He was astonished. "Want another beer?"

"No, no, that's okay . . . why don't you walk me home, and I'll give you a beer there?"

He nodded, the all-knowing smile stretching its way across his features. "I gotcha, lady." Tim reached over, and with the nonbeer-holding hand, ran his fingers across my thigh, just along the edge of my skirt. "You feel like a little company?"

Oh God, what was wrong with me? Why wasn't I ill? Why wasn't I running out of the bar before it was too late? Why did his words revolt me while the touch of his flesh against mine sent electric shocks all the way through my body? Why did this drunken guy, no different from every other drunk baseball-cap-wearing guy, make me mad with desire? Make me desperate for that hand to push its way up my thigh, and between my legs? Please, between my legs. Between my legs. Oh God.

I swallowed. "Yes. I want some company. You up for it?"

He laughed. "Am I ever. Let's fucking rock." He drained his beer in a matter of seconds, slammed the bottle onto the bar, gave the bartender a quick "see ya," and we were out the door.

It only took a minute before the regret kicked in. I think it was about halfway down the block, when I felt his arm around me, his body leaning against mine in that way drunken people do, his breath against my ear—I'm okay all through this—and then he licked me—and that's where he lost me. He licked my neck and the bottom half of my ear, and I cringed. It was so clumsy, so contrived, so awkward, so bullshit, so not the real romance I wanted, as far away from flowers and dinners and conversations as I could get, that when we got to the door to my building, I started with the excuses.

"Hey, Tim, I'm sorry, I just realized I'm really tired, and this isn't a good idea. I'm sorry to make you leave the bar, I definitely owe you a drink next time, but I really should just get to bed—"

His words, even though drawled in a slow, easy manner, cut into mine as severely as if they'd been delivered via knife. "You know, you talk too much."

"What?" I stared at him.

He laughed. "You talk too much. Sometimes you just got to be quiet, you know?"

Right. I nodded. Okay. Time to try again.

"Tim, I really got to get to bed. How about we meet tomorrow or something?"

He just stared at me. "You've got great eyes, you know?"

I blinked, not sure how to respond to a cliché I'd heard a million times before but never quite in this context, but then Tim took care of that. He opened the door to my building and held it open for me. I walked in hesitantly. He walked in behind me.

"Tim, I—"

I stopped suddenly as Tim suddenly shoved me up against the wall, and I couldn't exactly talk, what with his tongue in my mouth, one hand on my breast, the other on my hip. For the first couple of seconds, it didn't feel half-bad. And then it started to feel really good.

Really good.

Oh God.

He was pressed up against me with an urgency so intense, I couldn't believe the wall wasn't caving in around me. I couldn't believe I was still standing, pressed up against him as hard as I was. It was like gravity had nothing to do with it, we were somehow intertwined in our own particular body combination, being held up and tied down through the current of pure physical need.

And I needed more.

I was leaking down to the floor, my nipples practically cutting holes in my shirt, and his cock, through the layers of underwear and fabric, felt a million miles away.

"Come on, let's go upstairs," I stammered, trying to push him away from me.

"Fuck it. We're doing it here."

Almost with one motion, and I still can't figure out how he did it, because I think one hand stayed on my breast the whole time, his pants were open, my underwear halfway down my thigh, and the buttons from my shirt scattered on the floor as my nipples pressed their way toward the warmth of his mouth and the sharpness of his teeth.

Then, with a violent thrust, he was inside me, and I was right—I was split in two, but not with pain, with sensation, with his cock somehow pressing its way against my lungs, taking over my body like some arrogant conqueror and my body succumbing beneath him, desperately asking to be plundered. He was hard, he was fast, he was deep, everything I expected, everything I imagined, everything I feared, but still more. He was sweet and warm. He kissed me and he licked me and touched me and tasted me, and he bit my nipples until they turned red, then he sucked them until I begged him to stop and kiss me, instead. When he kissed me, it was almost like we'd been doing it forever, the way his tongue seemed to know the corners of my mouth, and my mouth seemed to relish the invasion.

Thank God I wore heels, and I dug those heels into the ground, the extra height giving me the perfect angle in which to curve myself against him, to press the end of his cock against my G-spot, close to perfection, close to heaven, close to everything you feel right before orgasm when you know you've never felt like this, and you wonder if you ever will, again.

He panted while he thrust, and it didn't smell like alcohol. It didn't smell like anything. I couldn't smell anything. I couldn't think. I could just dig my heels and curve and press and beg him to go harder, and his fingers pinched my nipples and sent waves of pleasure from my breasts to my clit and back again, then he reached his other hand down to my clit and started to rub, in slow circles, and I couldn't stand it anymore.

Between the circles and the thrusting and the pinching and licking, oh God, I fell against him, as he fell against me, and gravity was again defied, and it was just bliss and pleasure and waves and waves of orgasm and desire, and I laughed while I wanted to cry, and I didn't know how I was still standing, or if I even was, really, and he held me and we both became one being, somehow, full of heaving chest and sweat and his cum leaking down the edges of the condom which I hadn't even remembered being put on, but thank God someone was responsible, and thank God no one had come in the hallway, and thank God no one had heard us or seen us or—oh shit, I was starting to think again.

But then he saved me from myself. He slipped his hands between my legs.

"You're still wet," he said—and I was, I was wet all down my thighs.

I slipped my hand between his legs.

"You're still hard," I said—and he was, like nothing had happened yet, like he'd been wanting me for days in a buildup of frustration and desire, and that made me want him even more.

"Want to go upstairs?"

I grinned. "Sure. Come on up."

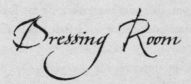

Dressing Room

The elevator could have fit four, which was good because it left the two of us with plenty of room to look at each other. I stared at him while keeping up my end of the conversation, wondering who this guy was who would just start talking to a girl like me in front of a bookshop elevator.

(I don't look like the kind of girl who shops for books, I look like the kind of girl who shops for leather.)

We rode up and down—level one to level three—as he tried to persuade me that I didn't need the book, and I tried to keep the words coming out of his mouth just long enough to get him to reveal his secrets.

(I didn't get the book, and I still haven't found his secrets, but I did get part of what I wanted.)

Three times in the elevator was two times too many,

and I wasn't really listening to what he was saying, since I'd long given up on his words telling me what I really wanted to know, and I had a meeting on Tottenham Court Road, so I told him it was time for me to go.

I gave him my card under the pretext of some video he was going to track down for me, figuring I'd never see him again. The secrets would be lost forever, and it would remain one of those moments that only hint at the potential between superficial chance encounters.

Life trains us for an endless habit of acceptance, of why bother. Slightly extended eye contact, an accidental bump in a crowded hallway, a shared smile on a subway, a conversation on an elevator ride—little moments where our universe collides briefly with another's, a glimmer of potential fusion—then separation as we fall back into the rhythm of our lives. We are lucky if we even remember to wonder what might have been.

Except that he did e-mail me. He had tried to track down the video, he hadn't lost my e-mail, and he'd remembered to write. He sat down in front of his computer and pressed send in my direction.

An effort by one human being to connect with another, even if under the guise of professional courtesy. It still counts, and I was pleased. I wrote back.

It gets tricky here, because I don't live in London. I was only there by chance—well, not chance really, since chance has so little to do with these things—I was there because of a photo shoot and a DJ and a lover who'd gone off to Prague with a girl from his past and hadn't bothered to call. And I was on the third floor of Foyles Bookshop because of Michael Alig.

I was supposed to have gone to London in March, but the plane reservation got screwed up, so I went back to my flat in Berlin, instead. But I didn't want to sit in Berlin while the boy I liked went off to Prague with a girl he'd once fancied.

What choice did I have, really? I was going mad in my flat. I had to get out of town, and I didn't like feeling like I couldn't get my own way, so London called—and that's how I ended up there for a quick visit, with the photo shoot rescheduled for Thursday and a DJ meeting for Wednesday at five, and me at Foyles, shortly before, looking for my book.

The first two bookstores didn't have anything on Michael Alig, my current obsession. It was only Foyles that had one of the books I wanted, and on the third floor, so up I went, and there it was. My book. Only, after flipping through, I wasn't so sure it was what I wanted after all. There wasn't so much about Michael, creative nightclub genius, but more about Michael, drug user/dealer, and New York clubs as drug distribution centers, and Miami, as an accompanying member of the industry.

I didn't care too much for that kind of gossip or historical narrative, so I debated, book in hand, while I waited for the elevator to come and collect me.

"Did you find the book you wanted?"

I looked up. A tallish boy had entered my elevator. Short,

dark blond hair. Blue eyes. Serious face. The kind of person you wouldn't be surprised to see in a bookshop, but the kind of person you would be surprised to see talking to me.

"Yes," I replied, gesturing to the book in my hand, already turning away. Who likes elevator conversations, anyway?

But then I decided that I did, actually. Especially when they are with nice boys who look thoughtful and don't reek of alcohol. I was also touched that he'd taken the initiative to speak with me, since something about being six feet with tattoos and Brigitte Nielsen hair usually scares most of the men away.

I figured I should offer a little more encouragement.

So I explained about the book. I explained about me and Michael Alig. I explained why I still wasn't sure if this book was really what I wanted. We rode up and down while I kept talking as an excuse to get him to keep answering. He helped me decide not to get the book, and we rode up one last time to replace the book, then back down to exit the bookshop.

I found out a little bit about him and told him a little bit about me—after all, we had run out of things to say about Michael Alig—and I had to go meet a DJ, and he had somewhere to go in the opposite direction, so he left, with my card, and I left, with a big grin on my face.

(Girls like me don't often get picked up in bookshops.)

I still didn't think much of it, partly because these sorts of things never really go beyond the level of anecdotal entertainment (how many lasting relationships do you know that started in an elevator?) and partly because when people say they'll e-mail you, they so rarely do.

But he did write (and he claimed he'd tried to find the video), and plans to meet were made for my next trip over.

When that day arrived, I felt positively teenager-ish with excitement, and when he called to figure out exactly when and where we should meet, all I could think was that I'd never heard anyone's voice sound so good on the telephone.

(Was I fifteen or what?)

It made me realize that I couldn't even remember exactly what he looked like, but I could have fallen in love with just the voice. It felt like slipping naked between the softest silk sheets, drowning in a warmth that coated itself around you. I stammered awkwardly on the phone, willing the voice to keep talking just so I could listen to it.

I couldn't remember the last time anyone made me act like this.

The original plan had been to meet at around 1:00 A.M., at my show that night, but then he had time earlier, and I had time earlier, so we agreed to meet at 10:00 P.M., just outside the original bookshop with the elevator.

I kept telling myself not to expect a lot from the whole thing. I mean, who was this guy? Some kid from a bookstore? I was sure he'd run for the door as soon as he saw me onstage, and that's if he was even able to handle my conversation beforehand.

(My usual dates involve guys who are more interested in

finding the bottom of their martini glass than in worrying about conversation highlights.)

Still, part of me couldn't help but think how wonderful it would be if at least it worked, if, maybe, bookish boy fell in love with a girl like me, and if maybe, then, I'd stop feeling so alone?

Stop it. Pull yourself together. Get yourself under control. I knew Expectations were dangerous. I'd been burned too many times to expect happiness to come from the hands of a guy. I knew better than that. I stood outside the bookstore, waiting for him, and told myself to grow up.

But wouldn't you know, it was just like a Lifetime movie. A regular Hallmark moment from start to finish. Astonishingly enough, considering how little time we'd spent together, our energies clicked as we kissed each other a quick hello. I slipped my arm through his, and off we went, as though we'd been doing this every night of our lives.

As though we were Tom and Jane out for a night on the town while the sitter put the kids to bed.

Talk about surreal.

I didn't know who I was, I'd never felt like this before. I'd never acted like this before. I felt like I was going through the motions, but somehow those motions felt more real than anything that had come before. How was that possible? I must have been playing a role, but whose?

We'd walked about half a block before I stopped, pulling him around to face me, and kissed him properly. I wanted to taste him. I wanted to make him real. I wanted to make this all feel more real. I wanted him close. To my pleasure and reassurance, and yes, also to my surprise as I'm still a jaded bitch, it felt right.

I guess we're never too old to become someone new?

I couldn't stop looking at him. I wanted to have my body touching his, even if it was just arm against arm or hip against hip. I hadn't been able to remember what he'd looked like in the bookstore, so all my pessimistic tendencies had come into play, but for no reason. The boy was attractive. It wasn't even the kind of attractive that I could convince myself was hot because his personality was so great. No, the boy was ATTRACTIVE—not to mention sweet, and charming (which I'd sort of remembered, but my God, ten minutes a month earlier isn't much to go on), even though he was completely different from the type of men I usually found myself holding hands with, or precisely because he was different.

(Need I mention that he was wearing a suit jacket?)

It felt funny to feel like I knew him as well as I did while not really knowing him at all. I felt complete with his energy, but his body was still unexplored terrain, if that makes any sense. And God, every part of my body wanted to touch and discover his. I still felt fifteen, a mess of nerves and tingly excitement.

It was even all right to have him at the club with me. I worried that he would hate it, that the music would be annoying, that there'd be too many people, that he'd get bored, that (even worse) he'd get dismissive, but no—he seemed perfectly at ease, and even somewhat entertained.

Just knowing that he was waiting for me, that his hand was there, at the end of his arm, for me to grab and hold and touch, that I could just walk over to him and kiss him, that I could wrap my arms around him and feel him, and that he was there, for me—that was all I wanted.

Of course, I had to pretend he wasn't there during my performance. I painstakingly kept my head turned to the right or the left, my eyes above his head, and I don't know if I ever stopped thinking, he's watching me, oh God, what is he thinking, but the show still went well, and he was there, after, to sit beside me and wait for me to finish what I had to finish, and he was there to leave with me and take me home with him.

Only I couldn't possibly wait for that.

Only I wasn't ready to go home yet.

Only I was still myself, even behind the schoolgirl nerves.

"I've just got to change," I said.

"I'll wait," he replied, motioning to a seat against the wall.

"No. Come with me."

I grabbed his hand and pulled him behind me into the dressing room. I'd been wanting to do this all night.

He was leaning against the door when I slid my hand behind him, feeling the door latch beneath my fingers. He looked at me, startled. Poor little academic boy. Brigitte was back in town.

I laughed to myself. Oh, but this was his mistake for ending up with a girl like me. I could be smart and well-read as much as the next girl, but I also liked to get a bit messy, and he'd better be able to handle a little dirt.

"Can I help you get your things together?" he asked, nervously.

"Yes. That was exactly what I had in mind," I said, not shifting position.

"Just tell me what to do," he said, trying to move away from the door, toward the clothes on the couch.

"No," I answered, shaking my head, reaching forward with one hand and pressing him back against the door. "You stay there. I need you to help me change my clothes."

He blinked. "Uh, okay." He paused while he waited for instructions, which were not forthcoming.

"What should I do?"

"Take them off."

He blinked again. I smiled. He really was very cute. I leaned over, sort of falling against him as he fell against the door. I wanted to feel his chest against mine, his thighs against my legs. For the library type, his body was perfect. For any type, really, his body was perfect.

Our faces inches apart, we stared at each other.

And then he kissed me. Oh, blessed proactivity! Even shy boys make a move every once in a while. There was hope yet. I felt the delicious sensation of his lips on mine, his tongue in my mouth, so soft, so sweet, so delicate, and I lingered there for a moment, while he wrapped his arms around me, and I stayed there, feeling his breathing, so caught up in the moment, I almost didn't notice that he unbuttoned my jeans and started to slide them off.

Except of course, that I couldn't help but notice, as the cold air of the dressing room struck my skin and made the heat coming off his body that much more conspicuous.

Little bookish boy was making all the moves here. I hadn't expected that.

"You're not so shy, are you?" I looked him in the eyes.

He grinned at me.

We stood there and smiled for a minute, and I whispered in his ear, "Aren't you going to take your pants off, too?"

"Why don't you take them off for me?"

I laughed. Looks like Mr. Academic had a bit more attitude than I'd thought. This could be fun.

"All right," I said. "But you've got to go there." I pointed to the couch.

It had been so long since I'd had this, I wanted to make sure I got exactly what I wanted. I wanted to enjoy it, and I was going to make sure he'd never forget it.

I pulled his pants off and got down on my knees. I slipped his boxers onto the floor and ran my hands up his thighs. Library boy did have an amazing body. His thighs were slim and muscular, and he tasted delicious under my tongue.

I ran my tongue up his legs and between them, sliding his cock into my mouth and against the roof of my mouth. He was so hard, and as if that wasn't obvious enough a sign of his desire, the moan he made as he slipped into my mouth sent shivers through my body.

(The corruption of innocence is quite an aphrodisiac.)

I was going to make this good.

I pushed him as far as I could down my throat, and then slowly started moving back and forth, but ever so slightly, as the pressure of my lips tightened and loosened. While my mouth moved back and forth, I kept my tongue constantly going up and down, pressed against the ridge of his cock. While tongue and mouth kept moving in tandem, I slipped my hand around the base of his cock and clenched firmly around the skin, keeping it pulled tightly back to accentuate every sensation as I licked and sucked and pressed and pushed.

I let my rhythm slowly build until I could feel him slowly start to pulse along with me, then I released my hold, letting my hand slide down to cup his balls, opening my mouth, just enough pressure to keep the warmth, and breathed on his wet skin, tongue flicking the tip, while he squirmed.

(I knew this was the best party he'd ever been to. Michael Alig had nothing on me.)

And then, just when I knew he couldn't stand it a second longer, I slowly pulled myself up on top of him.

"Want me to keep going?" I asked.

"Oh God, yes, yes, please," he panted, his eyes shut, his cock sticking straight out at me.

"Open your eyes."

He opened them just as I put my hand around his cock again, running it along the outside edge of my pussy and against my clit.

"Or would you rather a little of this?"

All he seemed to be able to say was, "My. God."

What an introduction.

I curved myself against him, feeling him skirt my outsides, and, then, when I couldn't stand it anymore, I slipped down on top of him, thighs on either side of his waist, hands against the wall, my head above his shoulder, and his cock—oh, his cock was inside me as far as I could shove it. And shove it I did.

Up and down, up and down, while his hands circled my waist, pulling me closer to him every chance he got. I don't know who wanted to go deeper, but deeper we went. Deeper and deeper until we were moving so fast, my hands kept slapping the wall until I gripped the edge of the couch to keep my hold, my thighs pressed tight against his waist, hips thrusting, and then the poor boy had what might have been the best orgasm of his life, and then, even more surprisingly, I had the best orgasm of my life.

Who expected that? From a bookstore elevator?

"Can I keep you?" I asked, running my fingers along his arms, through his hair, down his face, trying to absorb every inch of skin, trying to detail the sensation of this perfect creature with the soft nature and the hard thighs.

"You got it."

I ran my hands behind his back and held him close to me, feeling his breathing match mine.

"Did you have a good time?"

He laughed. "Yeah, of course."

We were quiet for a minute.

Then, as though I hadn't figured it out already, he said, "I've never done this before. Thank you."

I smiled at him. "Thank you for letting me disrupt your life."

"You can tell I'm not very good at it." He smiled back.

"I'm back in London next month."

"Perfect, I'll be waiting."

And with that, I leaned back against him, feeling him still inside me, and started contemplating the possibilities. There was so much I could teach him.

AVON

978-0-06-124085-0
$13.95

978-0-06-112864-6
$13.95 ($17.50 Can.)

978-0-06-089023-0
$13.95 ($17.50 Can.)

978-0-06-078555-0
$13.95 ($17.50 Can.)

978-0-06-085199-6
$13.95 ($17.50 Can.)

978-0-06-081705-3
$13.95 ($17.50 Can.)